THE GLAMSHACK

A NOVEL

BY PAUL COHEN

7.13 BOOKS
2017

Printed and distributed by 7.13 Books. First paperback edition, first printing: June 2017

Cover design: James Ty Cumbie
Author photo: Julie Afflerbaugh

ISBN-10: 0-9984092-0-0
ISBN-13: 978-0-9984092-0-7

Library of Congress Control Number: 2017944226

This collection is available in a variety of electronic formats including EPUB for mobile devices, MOBI for Kindles, and PDFs for American and European laser printers.

www.713books.com

For my parents, whose belief in me as a writer has made all the difference; for my children, upon whose presence I depend; for David Relin, still my first reader; for John Reynolds, still my rock; for Rachel, forever.

AUGUST 11, 1999
GLAMSHACK

I STAND behind my double screen doors, surveying my swimming pool, my rosemary bushes, my oak trees, my blond grass and blue-flame sky. By the pool, in a wide clay pot, a hose coils. Around the pot lie abalone shells, not yet cleaned by ants, reeking of sea. Are they really so rich around here they don't have ants? Did I say mine? Hell, none of this is mine. I live rent-free in this posh pool house on this tilted forested estate an hour south of SF at the whim of a pitying Silicon Baron who is an old friend of the Conquistador, my pitying boss.

Behind me, draped in shadow, resides love's detritus--sour noodles, festering shrimp, turned wine, plundered sheets. Beyond the screens sprawls a feral heat. With my face against this metal mesh I stand caught in a vise of my own devising. All I can do is breathe. All I can do is see. Leaves. Green leaves floating on the steel-surfaced pool. How long have those snotty leaves been there? Less than three days. Three days ago, those leaves were not there. Three days ago was the last time I swam in the pool. I'd told Her I could do three laps underwater and surfaced at two-and-a-quarter, gasping, treading water, slowly rotating, trying to focus on a spot behind the diving board where once I'd locked eyes with a charismatic fox and saw only Her, reclining naked with page-turner in hand on bright deck chair at pool's sparky edge. Her foot flexed and orange toenails waved and—I recall these three days hence—I responded like bull to cape and hoofed it through the water, gripped the pool's warm stone lip, pressed down, and rose up (striating my shoulder muscles), and She lay book on breast and gazed not at me but at Her own deer hued body, at purple nipples lit from within, at snake-taut belly, and as Her loving gaze wrapped my loving gaze I licked Her big orange toe and next thing I recall I was standing naked on pool's lip with Her rough heels hard against my shoulder blades and we were fucking in the way that makes me feel good-- She told me once that the way that makes Her feel good is the way that makes me feel good--and She loved it, She was right, I was wrong. (Had I ever actually contested this point?) After a Teutonic orgasm—Ach!—She stood, striding inside, no tan lines marring that metronome ass. Thin doors snapped shut, slumbering bumblebees woke, and I followed, through the heated clamor of my bees, finding Her dressing in the bedroom whereupon I laid naked on heartless sheets, my body heavened by a fading sun.

My body: my hell.

She stood over me, clothed.

"Would it be inappropriate," I said, "to make love again?"

"You feel it deeply, don't you?" She sat on the bed, gazing down at me in a disturbingly maternal manner, and I thought: don't you feel it deeply? "So pretty, my Henry," She said, stroking my head. Then: "I have to go."

"To New Orleans?"

"Yes."

"To your fiancé?"

Her regal jaw tautened. Her lioness eyes widened, as if I'd crossed a line.

She said, "I have to know what it feels like with him now. I don't want to regret."

"You've had to go so many times."

"It won't be like falling off into an abyss this time."

"How do you know?"

"You'll be fine, Henry Folsom."

"I can take it and he can't. I'm the tough one. Is that what you think?"

"I like how you stay solid," She said. "Even through this."

"I'm not solid."

"Yes you are."

"I'm air."

"I'll see you in twelve days."

"I'm salt."

"I'm flying the redeye."

"Last chance."

"Tonight."

"Don't go."

"Twelve days."

I watched Her walk to Her car. She skipped past the agapanthus, past the pool. Fucking skipped. The little robot that cleans the bottom squirted at Her, and She dodged the stream. So graceful. I remember thinking that. Three days ago. She is the most graceful and strong creature I have ever encountered, I thought, and I love Her so much I am nothing, without Her. Without Her I am air I am salt I am fire I am back inside the Glamshack bringing the screen doors together like a penniless lord closing up the Great Hall after a barren feast, spearing a shrimp in the splotched steel pot on the counter, returning the unmolested orange corpse to its sullied silver crypt, taking a final cheap-ass wineglass by the porcelain-log fire, surveying my borrowed domain, plucking from the floor (with the limp wrist of the highborn) a black hardcover book on the Plains Indian Wars, placing a piece of white paper atop it, and writing Her a letter.

Fight and get burnt, I wrote. *Slump and go under. A Pleistocene world I inhabit now, all fire and swamp and monsters. Lord knows I don't blame you for removing yourself from this existence. There's nothing I want more than to leave it. But I can't leave it, or it won't leave me, until you and I are together again, or until I've moved through every cursed region, all the beautiful rooms, and they've become part of me. And I believe the above goes for both of us. Because we're commingled now, even when apart. It's like we're sailing the same vessel through separate seas. And what I know from this blessed vessel, these evil seas, is this: your skin is my sun, your pores my Pleiades. Through your golden eyes, I find phosphorescence where others see only black water; in your gaping absence a nightbreeze grazes my blood whenever I contemplate joy.*

Dusk releases me. I push through the screen doors onto the porch. The wind has worsened. Snakey clouds. A chill. Working up to a witchy night. Up there a deep-space bass grows. Like the whump of a stereo in a drug dealer's Mustang 5.0, only deeper. Three black helicopters flying in formation. Whumpsuck. The dusk flutters and fades; not even the sun can resist.

I sit on the porch's wood planks, hug my goosebumped legs, press my cheek to purpling knees. I've got to end this grisly business; I've got to get free of Her. But how? Travel far, far away? Hurtle into the arms of another woman? Slather my pathetic self in my own nauseating madness? *Slather my pathetic self in my own nauseating madness.*

That's it. That's what I'll do. From beginning to end.

So. Henry. How did this madness begin?

FEBRUARY 13, 1999
HOW IT BEGAN

IN A CAFE, of all boring places. He's looking at his notes from an interview he's just done with a woman who directs television commercials and once did a video for a famous rock star. Looking at, not reading his notes, for they fill only about a third of a page of lined legal paper, they're festooned with paper-piercing doodles. From these notes, he must come up with a two-thousand-word admiring profile for the weekly glamour magazine (heretofore referred to as the "Glamrag") that constitutes his bread and butter gig—Oh, O.K., his only gig.

Problem was he hated this woman, and she hated him. If it wasn't hate at first sight, certainly they were hating one another within five minutes of meeting. She was blond, thin, well into middle age, with eyes in that surgically instilled state of perpetual surprise and on her head was a turban. *A turban.* In tow she had a smaller, younger, blonder and prettier woman who turned out to be her Rep and who was getting no play from the patrons in the presence of her astonished, behatted boss.

"What's your ideal crew," he had asked her at some point in the disastrous interview. Then, as if to distract himself from the impending embarrassment, he glanced at the Rep and thought: worth a shot?

Turban Lady looked at him, surprised. "My ideal crew?"

The Rep looked down. All film crews have the same makeup. Henry knew this, but he'd never taken the time to find out what that makeup was or what the various crew members did. What was the point? Film was a silly business. A film, so Henry often told people, could never be art.

"Two grips," she said, as if speaking to a child. "A gaffer."

There was no turning back. She would list the members of a film crew for him, and he would listen and take notes as if this was a scoop. He crossed his legs European style.

Afterward, from a payphone, he called his editor, a fallen Conquistador who routinely took Henry out for drinks and at check-time confessed to being broke, to commiserate, only to hear that Turban Lady already called this editor to demand a different interviewer. How did she get to a phone so fast?

Cell phone, Henry realized, white-knuckling the receiver. Cell phone and Turban.

"She said you didn't know what a gaffer was," the Conquistador told him. "She said you were incompetent and rude."

"I quit," Henry responded. "I hate these people."

Back at his table, while perusing his notes (which read, in total, in half-inch high letters: *Gaffer. Grip.*), he encounters a voice.

"Are you an actor?" says the voice.

He looks up to see a flower in a clear plastic cup on his table. Above the flower, She gazes radiantly down.

"You were an actor," She says.

"No, I was…"

He is the only man on earth. It's not that he rivets Her gaze. Simply nothing seems of interest to Her in this cafe—in this world—but his face. She cocks Her head, smiles, and Her smile is a projection, it doesn't occur physically, on Her face, it happens all around the two of them. Her smile is…an Event. Like falling on a knife while running through woods. Like fire.

"Yes," he says, lying for no reason he can fathom. "I was."

"So was I."

"Stupid stuff."

"Is being a journalist stupid?"

"Stupider."

"That woman in the turban."

"Really fucking stupid."

"Oh," She says, "a table's opened up." And She plucks flower and cup and removes Herself from him. She does it cleanly, with an abruptness that leaves him stunned. In awe. Such a simple move, such a wallop, such purity of purpose, beast-like grace, absence of homage to anyone or anything but her own slick and sinewy… Grip.

Grip?

Grip as in this superfine woman, who just put a flower on my table and smiled everywhere but on the kisser and who is now sitting two tables away reading a scholarly book on cruel and unusual punishment, has a grip on me; *grip* as in what Turban Lady said grip meant (what did she say grip meant?).

Gaffer.

Gaffer as in if you don't make hay out of this one, buddy, this will be the biggest gaffe the world has ever seen and you deserve to float in hell; *gaffer* as in you are a big fucking gaffer for quitting your job when, let's face it, your job and your good looks are all you've got going for you in the world.

On his way to the phone, he passes Her, and She does not look up.

"It's Henry."

"We've got someone else lined up to do the interview," the Conquistador says.

"Who?"

"Me."

"You're an…editor?"

"I'm a man. I deal with a situation. I don't pinch my nose and roll my eyes and wish things were different. Hell, even a high school kid knows he's got to do his homework. What's a gaffer?"

"I just met this woman."

"And then you pissed her off. The fucking director of a Prince video. We're a glamour rag not *The New York Times*."

"No, a different woman."

"You stay away from her rep. She's married to a producer."

"She's not the rep. She's…"

She's watching him. He stands, phone in hand, watched. Is that what sucks the poor boy in? The watching? A parched sailor, he can't help but lift his head.

"Henry, what's a gaffer?"

"Me."

"Ha Ha."

"If I don't get off this phone and make hay, I'm a gaffer."

"That woman?"

"She's enchanting. I'm enchanted."

"That's good. You go make hay, I'm off to do an interview."

"I didn't mean it. When I said 'I quit.' I didn't mean it."

"No shit."

Passing back to his table, She looks up and fills the cafe with smile. He stops.

"You're back," She says.

"Yes."

"What's your story about?"

"Oh, it's boring. What are you reading?"

"It's amazing. This writer, he actually makes you understand the mind and motivation of the torturer."

"Wow. How about coffee next week? Same place, same time?"

FEBRUARY 20, 1999
ENCHANTED MOMENTS

ALL SEAS, for some people, are stormy all of the time, and to live is to either search for a port or defend one. For others, skies loom blue and waters flick with vitality, and to live is to always be setting out for farther reaches. For Henry, seas are stormy most of the time, yet he continuously sets sail in the worst of weather and winds up clinging to the mast, eyes scrunched shut, praying to a God he wants desperately to believe in while at the same time, thumping his chest as if to say there is no God but me. Three things may happen at this juncture: wind worsens and Henry's poor craft is tossed closer and closer to the edge of the world and helpless and terrified, he sails on; clouds part, sun shines, Henry shinnies down from the top of the mast, dashes below for a captain's suit and sword, dashes back up and strides his solitary vessel like a goddamn conquistador (fucking A right, I'm a god!); wind subsides, waves too, Henry opens his eyes to find himself in a harbor which he wants never to leave but alas, it is one of those man-made things, like the one they constructed for D-Day, and eventually, inevitably, it gets blown to smithereens and Henry almost gets blown to smithereens with it, but manages to escape with a leaky craft and a rusty sword into enemy waters. If there is a default state, or equilibrium, it is a stormy sea, a ghost ship, a company of one.

She is not a harbor.

She is a sea.

There sits the sea.

There sits the sea wearing bell-bottom jeans and high-heeled sandals and one of those fuzzy sweater tops that shows Her belly. In the café. At the appointed time—exactly one week from the act of placing a flower on his table. What a belly. A sea of belly.

Bellysea.

Henry sits.

"Let's get out of here," he says.

She looks at him, smiling beatifically. "O.K."

So easy he wonders what the catch is.

She stands, pivots away from him, bends to fetch a red backpack. *Oh boy.*

So what's the catch?

They wander to a green spot in a park. Henry has brought along books. He's marked passages to read to Her--bold, biblical-sounding prose that stirs the passions and paints Henry as a spirited darkhorse. They sit on a stone wall and She dangles Her feet. As Henry reads he can feel it working. He can see it on Her face. She looks as if She's just eaten a warm muffin. When he finishes, She says, "Mmmmm."

Her smile lingers in the sunshiny air. Henry says something about how he's going to bilk Hollywood. "I'm doing it for the fucking money," he says. She laughs. A student of torture, She says She finds Henry refreshing. She doesn't actually say it, but Henry picks up on this (remember, "I'm not completely stupid"). He runs with this-- the real world guy, not above a bit of grubbing to get a seven-course meal, no stranger to throwing a punch either. *Fuck that shit's what I say.*

She says three guys sat at Her table before Henry showed up. Strangers.

"What is it about me?" She says. "Do I look like I want men to sit at my table?"

"You look..."

What is it about Her particular brand of loveliness that turns old Henry to tapioca? She's not delicate featured, not in the least. She's got a big, strong jaw, hands that are almost manly, packaged cleavage and lioness hair. The hands remind Henry of his mother's, no-nonsense, get-the-job-done hands. The jaw and cleavage and hair play superbly with the bearing, which is unhurried, regal, bemused. Her manner is this: you tickle me mildly. And—and this is what turns old Henry to tapioca—She seems to need enchanted moments as much as He does. What's more, She seems to see enchantment in him. Which makes old Henry feel downright lovely. Even divine.

"Have you heard of the Century Foundation?" She says.

"No."

"Good."

"Why good?"

"You're too natural for that."

"What is it?"

"I don't want to ruin you."

"You already have."

Three pointer! The jaw dips, the mane tumbles, the cleavage pouts, and for square miles a man would encounter nothing but Her shy smile.

"Actually," says Henry, "I'm irruinable."

"Irruinable?"

"Means—."

"I can guess. You call yourself a journalist?"

"Not really."

"What then?"

"Tell me about the Century Foundation. And be specific please."

Hook shot! So She digs a smartass. No doubt She's sick of men puddling at Her feet.

Mental note: No puddling.

"The Century Foundation is a three-day seminar where you identify the things that hold you back from achieving your full potential. Then you squash them."

She looks at him soberly and he shrinks inside.

She laughs. "I'm kidding. I mean that's the idea, I guess. I know so many people who've done it. Sounds kinda spooky. Like squashing bugs inside of you."

"People aren't that simple."

"No."

"People are full of things you can't explain. You wouldn't want to explain a lot of things inside people. You never…" A cloud—really!—dissipates and sunlight descends in a soft sheet. Henry notices that the pores in Her face are bigger than he'd ever seen in a woman before. The sun turns Her honey color to berry. The trinity of trees before them possesses, in the green of its leaves, the essence of light. Now he, Henry, natural man, magic man, darkhorse extraordinaire, rivets her enchanting/enchanted gaze.

"…Ever want to kill the unknowable."

Jaw dip, mane tumble, ball swishes, crowd sounds.

Dinner, my house, this weekend?

She'd love to but She'll be in New Orleans this weekend.

Dinner, my house, next weekend?

She'd love to.

AUGUST 13, 1999
GLAMSHACK

WHAT STINKS? Abalone shells? Skunk? Fox? My pathetic existence? Her pathetic existence? The fiancé's pathetic existence? The fucking going on right now in the 700-square-foot New Orleans Love Nest (jointly owned, no doubt, by Her and the fiancé) with the lion fountain in the courtyard outside? This business of re-living does not seem to be going the way I'd planned. It does not seem to be freeing me from Her. Is it too early to expect a small sign of progress? Why do I believe, still, after all Her lies, after barely surviving Her mineral ability to cleave Herself in two—one for me, one for the fiancé; a kiss for me, a sweaty anal session for the willowy, drawling chump—after all the betrayals, why do I continue to believe She is not intent on ruining me? And—this is the kicker—why can't I spasm off the notion that something in Her recognizes something in me; that something in us is the same?

On the porch, in my chair, I grip my empty wineglass, study the robot napping on the bottom of the pool. The shrimp. Still uneaten in the pot inside. The shrimp stink.

I stand. Look up. Spot a contrail in the backlit sky and try to trace it to its source but, it seems, there is no source. It would be death to accept this as symbolic so I go inside, refill the glass, return to the porch. When was the first betrayal? Her Birthday? I didn't know about the fiancé on her birthday. I thought She was visiting friends. She told me that. In the café. The next day she was on a plane, to New Orleans. To the fiancé. The enemy.

A mad thought: the fiancé could help. If I grit my teeth and conjure this first betrayal—the horror, the horror—perhaps it will help me get free. Did he meet Her at the airport? Was there a party? Was there a fucking party?

Of course there was a sweaty fucking party.

MARCH 1, 1999
THE FIRST BETRAYAL

THOUGH SHE has never been told this, She knows Her fiancé has been working on the party for weeks. He's good at parties, at assembling people and creating ambiance for the sole purpose of pleasing Her. His genius is in his ramshackle elegance, a graceful indifference. He makes it seem as if She were simply being honored with casual admittance to his world, a world that grinds with the ghetto, high-fives the frat boys and tips its hat to the wellborn. *Glad you could make it, wouldn't miss a beat if you didn't for as you can see, the beat here goes on and on.*

She pierces eastward, fleeing a downing sun. Dry riverbeds fill and flow over. A darkening desert. She catches Herself holding Her breath, waiting for the absolute. Dark. It spreads fast, like a parachute popping on Her funnycar thoughts. She exhales, side-eyes the man in the neighboring seat. The laptop. Lapdog. He catches Her eye, smiles. Yuck. Why are they all so pathetically easy? Monochromatic midgets. He turns back to the terminal screen and She suddenly feels ashamed and abandoned. What did She do wrong to make him abandon Her like that? Can he see inside? Easy, She thinks. She thinks: he knows nothing. He's worth nothing. He wants to rut Her like all the rest. Then parade Her. But why did he turn away? What's wrong with Her? Is She…unattractive?

"If I had to squeeze by you to use the girls room," She says, "would you have to quit your application first? I'd hate to make you do that."

"My application. Um, no. I'd just…I'd save. Would you like to…? Do you, um…?"

Turn up smile, look in eyes, hold head cocksteady. Say: "Do I…?" and watch male seize up, as if "Do I" were "I Do." Substory: The Entire Universe.

"I admire anyone who can work on an airplane," She says.

"You do?"

"I enter a kind of gray, suspended state. I can't work, I can't sleep. I have this book, it's fascinating, it actually makes you understand the mind and motivation of the torturer. And I can't read it, I can't focus."

Spreadsheet succumbs to screensaver. He notices nothing but the smile coiling around his body like a python.

"I know what you mean," he says.

"But you focus."

"I've got to."

"I'll bet you're the boss."

"Well, a lot of people…"

"They depend on you, on your will. Your nerve."

"You can't imagine."

She leans into the crook between seat and window. Her hair seems to grow bigger, acquire a higher honey luster. She eases up on the smile, the squeeze.

"I admire you."

Spring night in New Orleans. Over the fields outside the terminal, the air chugs with winged industry, machines and insects, guess which will inherit the planet. Inside the terminal: segmented eternity. Inside the airplane, the seat belt sign pings. Passengers stumble hungrily into the aisle, lunge for overhead luggage as if suitcases were silverware, line up like conventioneers at a long-delayed buffet. A famished man chest-butts his way two aisles forward and opens a compartment. Her rose-print duffel punches his shoulder. He staggers back, striking women and children and not an apology in the offing. He returns to his seat, but doesn't sit. He clutches the rose-print bag in one hand, the encased laptop in the other. He stands in the aisle, blocking passage to all but Her.

She hasn't even begun to rise. She gazes up at him.

"You don't need to carry that," She says.

He says nothing.

The fiancé gathers Her at the airport. The scene with the three of them at the gate—Her, the fiancé and the man carrying Her bag—left Her with a familiar charge, neither positive nor negative, a color-coded life force from that third universe She inhabits. The man carrying her bag was suggesting a drink in a new French Quarter club when they ran smack into the willowy fiancé, who, to the man's astonishment, didn't bat an eye, simply took Her in his arms. The man watches them embrace and while he's being introduced, does not know whether to shake hands or how to do so with a bag in each hand. Fight and flight play a seething peekaboo with one another, and finally, because he's not completely crazy, flight wins.

She says, "Mmmm" at the sight and sound of the lion fountain in their courtyard, at the orchids She raised and he husbanded in Her absence, at the second-floor balcony outside their 700-square-foot bedroom.

At the door he sets down her rose-print bag, turns to Her and says, "Welcome home, baby." He kisses Her long and deep, then opens the door onto a roomful of folks rich and poor, many races, straight and gay, male and female and indeterminate. It's not like a sitcom surprise party where everyone has been crouching behind couches, and the fiancé has issued a pre-agreed signal upon arriving in the courtyard whereupon lights were doused and music silenced. No, the music plays, the lights light, and the people, most of them, don't even notice the door has opened. A few do and they stride forward to pinch at Her and nibble.

She remains just inside the entryway. Slowly, the party revolves toward Her. She can feel it happening and She will not progress any farther into the room until the revolution is complete. The fiancé has already slid, as expected, back into the nose-ringed women in slips sexed up over the soft spoken musicians; back into the fluted glasses overflowing with pink liquid and the song of a languorous female rapper trying to sound like Billie Holliday. He's put on this party for Her, he's put up with the man carrying Her bag and countless other men-carrying-Her-bags, he's putting up with his current expected slide away from Her, the toll on his soul levied by the effort at graceful indifference, because he knows that later tonight, unlike anyone else in this funky, fleshy room, he'll be fucking Her.

The Billie Holliday chick says: Boom, clack, boom, clack, boom. Time to stride.

AUGUST 13, 1999
GLAMSHACK

I WALK inside, refill my wine, walk back to the porch, pacing its length twice. I sit and sip and search the night sky for contrails but can't find one, and even if I could, I wouldn't be able to trace it for more than a second because I've lost focus. Does She really think in such narcissistic banalities as "Time to stride?" Isn't that what I want, to conjure Her as a woman who thinks in narcissistic banalities, and to allow those banalities to set me free? But what if, instead, She has thoughts like, "Thank God I'm home, and all my friends are around me and my husband-to-be is here, and the lion, that symbol of love, is still spouting water." What if, as the Billie Holiday chick closes out another grieving baby doll tune and the musicians have abandoned the slip women in favor of Her burgeoning presence and someone calls out, "Toast to…" What if She, of the mysteriously large pores, of the brutish irresistibility, embraces an old friend, clings tight, then walks not strides through the crowd carrying Her own valise and paying lip service to the slips and musicians, the straights and gays and indeterminates (for that is what the fiancé intended for them, lip service), and finds him where he laughs in a small throng and hooks an arm through his—he has intended this too, the disappearing and the finding. What if She guides him upstairs, saying to the others, "Y'all be patient, I've got to see about my man," and what if She experiences deep in her seabelly, as She ascends the spiral stairs with the fiancé on Her arm and the rose-print valise in Her no-nonsense hand a sudden turbulence, the flick of a whale's tail, at the thought of that spirited darkhorse in whose stall She will be dining the very next week?

MARCH 9, 1999
THE FIRST DINNER

"WHEW," She says. "You've got steep narrow stairs, Henry Folsom. Is that a test?"

"I like to think of my stairs as a passageway."

"To what?"

"To a sea."

"Mmm."

Henry presses his back against the wall. It seems he can do nothing wrong. Where's the catch?

She steps past him, Her panther jaw, Her sinewed sandaled feet, Her fierce calves and fighting breasts. She resounds down the hall with such confident grace that the observer uninitiated in the subterranean ways of this incandescent being would think this was Her home when, in fact, this evening, this Dinner, marks Her inaugural encounter with the Lighthouse.

Henry, offhandedly, palms shut the door, watching her stride toward the dwelling's center.

Unlike the fiancé, of whose existence Henry is at present unaware, Henry is not a conjurer of atmosphere. For apparel he has donned the usual: jeans, boots, t-shirt. For furniture he owns but one chair and this given to him by a buddy who moved across the sea. Wall hangings consist of a set of stone age arrows, also bestowed by the absent friend, and a dive knife. Pull-out couch, black lounge chair, particleboard bookcases, spindle-legged kitchen table, these belong to Lighthouse owner who resides across the hall and intends to evict Henry and convert his abode into a master bedroom for his burgeoning family.

And yet, in his own way, Henry's done the fiancé proud. The apartment feels like the pilot house in an old oceangoing fishing vessel, with an attached deck to boot. Or the command room in a storm-wracked lighthouse in Newfoundland. Henry the keeper of the flame. Beacon for All Out There in the Dark. This, he hopes, is how She experiences this place. One of deep warmth. Of magic.

For this evening, he's purchased phosphorescent-pink hunks of tuna each shrink-wrapped in plastic. Basmati rice. Living lettuce. Candles.

She would never guess he's not magic.

She suggests eating the tuna raw.

The fish shines like an excised organ. They stand over it, watching.

"It's beautiful," She says.

He says, "I heard they mate for life, tuna."

"We could be eating somebody's husband."

"Wife."

"If anybody's gonna get netted," She says, "it's the husband."

"Actually," says Henry, "it might have been sea bass that mates for life."

He slices off a hunk. It parts willingly from the main. Henry pours soy sauce into a bowl and sprinkles in coarse ground pepper. He's never done this before, but as he twists the cap back on the pepper he can feel the sure hand of God on his.

Hands Her the hunk.

"Yours."

She takes fish between forefinger and thumb. She is looking at him while She does this. Four, five…The ceremony of Accepting the Fish from Henry is complete. She turns Her attention to the bowl. Henry has placed short, squat scented candles on the sturdy white table behind them. Many candles. Lit for one half hour before She arrived. Brown and red candles, they have lovelied the scratched white wood with their wax. They provide the only light in the Lighthouse. Through the arched doorway—there are no doors in the apartment, only arches—the dining room/bedroom/living room/study waits like the long night to come.

Here in the kitchen, dusk lingers. In this gray glimmer, the soy sauce acquires an inky depth, and vibrating shadows hone Her already brutal jaw. She wears an elegant peasant's shirt, low cut with flecks of color and a silky sheen billowing. Beneath it, Henry senses the belly, the snakelike tautness. Her breasts suggest another animal. The lit-pink meat is pushed into the bowl, under the inky surface until only Her gripping fingers remain, flecked with sauce, capable. Pause, remove. Dipping the Fish becomes Loving the Fish. She does not close Her eyes. This is a woman who does not close Her eyes while She is Loving the Fish. The effect is exhilarating and tense. For long after She swallows She says nothing, expresses nothing. Henry knows better than to ask a question; tastes vulgar and ethereal swim through Her senses, and he is convinced, at this stage in the ceremony, that only She has the grace and courage to experience them all.

She takes the knife from Henry and cuts him a hunk. She repeats the process only this time, She feeds our man. He mimics Loving the Fish. He believes he experiences all those tastes because it is Her he is with, Her he has learned from. (Eating has never been a social event for Henry, nor an artistic one.)

"Mmm," he says, and immediately regrets having cheapened the ceremony with such a common response.

"People don't know how to eat," She says.

"No," says Henry, "they don't."

"They miss the ritual."

"They do."

"They miss so much."

"I know."

"I love that you know how to eat."

She says this and looks him in the eye.

He says, "I know how to eat."

They carry the table, candles and all, into the living room/bedroom/diningroom/study. Henry grills one of the tuna steaks and they share it. Wine. They don't touch the salad.

"We've made a place," She says.

And She's right, and it's wondrous, this place that used to be Henry's homeless apartment. This place he'd now rather inhabit than any place on earth. He can hear the creak of the iron cosmos lid. Lifting. And the light in this place. Dusky as the Dark Woods, and as thick with desire. The same desire for Henry at thirty-three as for Henry at ten. The same desire. For a recognition. Of something just out of reach. Though both Henry at thirty-three and Henry at ten feel the hairs of a silent roving, both hear faintly the incantation toward conflagration, both see…

Candles down to ancient volcanic cones, firelight on lettuce, plates licked by wax. They sit at opposite ends of the table, Henry and Her, and between them lies Italy. The kitchen and the bathroom: other countries. The Balkans, Azerbaijan. Windows: inland seas.

On the couch, they smoke a joint She brought. Henry's not a pot smoker. He doesn't like the way it makes him inward and obsessive. It doesn't do that now. He puts his hand on Her leg. They kiss.

"Sounds cheesy," says Henry, "but maybe we should pull out the bed."

"It doesn't sound cheesy," She says. She sits with back straight, no-nonsense hands clasped churchily in her lap. "It's practical."

On the deck, they sit on a short bench, wrapped in a blanket, naked. He is still wrangling with the image of Her walking from his bed to the bathroom. This came from my bed. This drowsy predator. Sated, for now. Henry's redwood rises beside them, shields them from a bone-chip moon. Four stories below lie lovingly tended gardens flushed with color, dark now, invisible. You have to take it on faith, and we do, he does, that they are magic, these gardens.

The back-building neighbor's year-round Christmas lights titter like cherubs at the scene on the deck; how they rejoice at mortal joy. Henry wants to say something about how these lights resemble mini-angels but he's worried she'll think he's weird, so instead he says the first stupid thing that comes to mind.

"I always wanted to be an Indian," he says. "In elementary school, junior high too. I'd get off the bus one stop early and run through the woods to my house. One day a week, the day I was allowed to wear sneakers to school, gym day. I would pretend I was an Indian, and it made me run faster. One day, I ran by a couple fucking. He looked at me, and it scared the hell out of me, and I ran fast as any Indian ever ran. I was probably thirteen or fourteen. Always was a late bloomer. You know I had baby teeth in college?"

"Why?"

"Why did I have baby teeth in college?"

She giggles.

"Why was I scared? Because they were, uh, fucking."

"Why did you want to be an Indian?"

Henry snorts an un-cherubic laugh. "I don't know. Actually I do. But it's hard to explain. And embarrassing."

"More embarrassing than fucking?" She says.

"I…" He looks at his blanketed crotch. Is fucking embarrassing? Perhaps it is. Perhaps he never noticed. He should notice things like this, he thinks. Then he says something grand-sounding, something along the lines of: one day, the Indians were breathing freedom and mystery the way they'd done for centuries—the way we breathe air—and the next, that freedom and that mystery were being sucked from their magic atmosphere by a horde of white bugs invading from the east, and soon the Indians were, as are all of us now in this tragic almost-post-millennial world, confronted with a choice between martyrdom to mystery—to magic—or the soul-shriveling process of evolution, of de-magification, though truth be told Henry does harbor the hope that a tribe, a band, even just one brave, secretly managed to light upon a third way; to discover deliverance.

She is looking and smiling at him with her head cocked a quarter turn. "When I was fourteen," She says, "my dad came on to me for the first time."

"Oh," says Henry. "Really."

"He's homeless now," She says, "and a paranoid schizophrenic. He sleeps in his car sometimes in my mother's driveway. They've been divorced since I was five. He loved pancakes. He still loves pancakes. I used to beg my mom to make pancakes and pretend to eat mine, and later I'd slip out the door and serve him through the window."

"Of his car," Henry says.

"Of his car," She says. "With syrup and, once in a while, strawberries. I did it for years, until I moved away to college."

"Your mother never caught on?"

"I don't know. She might have turned a blind eye. He was an amazing man. Is, amazing. His sight, his courage, they compel a kind of worship." And then She too says something grand-sounding (is it the influence of the cherubs?), something along the lines of Her father saw to the black-lava center of the world and he did not flinch at what he saw and the demons down there when they saw him seeing them and not only not flinching but singing, singing the theme song to curly-red Annie, the demons got furious and flew and landed on him and never left and because they landed on Her father—Her hero, Her lover, Her flesh—they landed on Her. They never left Her, either.

She turns toward Henry. In Her lioness eyes, a seething invitation: *Heal this.* The blanket slips off Her shoulder, Her sleek, smooth, brown, striated shoulder, and Henry suddenly loses the conversation's mad flow; he remembers only bits of what She just said. In order to say something to fuel the mad ecstatic flow, he says, "What kind of car?"

"What?"

"What kind of car? Did he sleep in? In the driveway?"

"Jeep Cherokee."

"I always wanted one of those."

"You've got a nice truck."

"It's got no power."

"In high school I went out with forty-year-old men. I almost became a high class prostitute. I didn't have any friends in college, and I had times if somebody spoke to me I'd just burst out crying. I don't know who I am. Or maybe I do." She inhales loudly. "Maybe I know exactly."

"Did you ever want to be an Indian?"

"I'm a quarter Cherokee."

Henry looks up from the shoulder. "And you let me go on like that? God how embarrassing. Boy, do I feel stupid."

"It's O.K. A lot of people want to be Indians."

"That supposed to make me feel better?"

"I don't know, does it?"

Henry glances at the neighbor's lighted cherubs. He is charmed near tears. He pulls Her in for a kiss, and this kiss, never before such a kiss, never have lips shifted from solid to sauce, never this puddling, in the brain, in the bones, and though he must know (somewhere) that puddling is a condition often ending in misery, he seems not to care for his lips are pressing a question into Hers: *Baby, what do you want?*

AUGUST 13, 1999
GLAMSHACK

DID I really hear the hallelujah creak of the cosmos lid lifting? That
First Dinner. That night of first fucking. Missionary, sure, but a
heathen missionary—fucking all night long and not at all proper
with Her veined hands gripping the erotic crease behind Her knees,
pressing them back nearly to Her shoulders, those grape-hued knees,
those shuddering muscled shoulders, rat-a-tat-tat, that jaw, those
pores, that…Sound. What is that sound?

That rattleclank sound.

I back through the screen doors into the Glamshack. Onto
the sea-blue carpet. The void-blue carpet. That sound. It's of the
selfsame cosmos lid, only now it's not lifting—it's settling into
position. Rattleclank. It's a sound that does not occur in the ear
but rather, like the event of Her smile (and so profoundly unlike
that event), happens everywhere. How can one entity produce
such absolutes of joy and emptiness? For that matter, how can
there exist, in one world, such a glorious event as the First Dinner
and such a profane being as the fiancé. It's not possible. Or it is
possible, which means everything is possible, which means there is
no such thing as value and all is madness. One thing for sure: I'm

getting no closer to freedom, to sanity, to living. Is there any other way to look at this business? Any other approach?

Rattleclank.

I shudder, and remember when I was ten and Danny was my best friend and we were playing with knives on a day such as this and he was talking about an escaped madman who dances around fires and down came the rattleclank and the next thing I knew I was running alone through the woods with two knives in hand looking for this mad bastard and though it's hard to know which of the acts that ensued were real, I realize that that day was the real day my madness began.

JUNE 7, 1976
HENRY AND THE MADMAN

THE DAY is warm and inert. Sun like a molten manhole cover. Sometimes the days are like this for Henry, even at ten. Even then, he hears the lid of the cosmos rattleclank into position.

Henry and Danny are out back of the house throwing knives at each other's bare feet. Mumbletypeg is the name of the game. The object is to aim for a near miss. The knives disappear into the clumpy grass that Henry's father rarely cuts—his is a family that pays little attention to appearances. His is a world of fundamentals: kindness, work, enriching activities, integrity. Below them, the grass slopes down to viney pine woods through which, on good days, Henry runs top speed and grinning. This is not a good day. For no specific reason.

"I saw on TV that a madman escaped," says Danny. "Ahh!"

Danny's leg spasms to avoid the wild throw Henry just launched. The knife bounces on a clump of grass.

"Henry!"

"What."

"I quit."

"You can't."

He doesn't.

Danny throws his knife and his throw is wide. Henry doesn't budge. Usually not budging as the knife sings footward is a frightful and thrilling experience ending in a triumph of the spirit. I didn't budge. The small brown handle—if the throw was a good one—sticks out of the ground like a Mayan monument. In a featureless yard of clumpy, yellowed grass. Something's happened.

This time, nothing. Henry pulls the knife from the ground, folds the blade, puts it in his pocket.

"What are you doing?" says Danny.

"Nothing."

"Gimme my knife."

"Why?"

"It's mine. You have three now and I only have one."

"You throw like a girl."

"Gimme it."

Henry thinks: Dinks. A name Danny hates. A benevolent despot, Henry doesn't say it. He reaches into his pocket for the knife, stops. He looks at Danny, the quivering lip.

"Where'd the madman escape from?" says Henry.

"A madman jail. Around here."

"What else?"

"He likes fires."

"Fires?" Inside his pocket, Henry thumbs the blade partway open.

"He dances around them."

"Really?"

"Y-Y-Yeah."

Henry brings out the knife. He opens the blade, It's so brightshiny that he can see his own face and it scares him. The lid of the cosmos begins to lift.

"Let's go," says Henry.

"Where?"

"Mission."

"What mission?"

"Find the madman mission."

Bumblebees tense against dogwood blossoms. Birdsound lonely as leaves floating on a swimming pool. Pine needles brittle with heat. Henry extends the knife toward his best friend.

"If you come with me," says Henry, "you can keep the knife."

Danny studies it. He steps back. "No."

A hot flush rushes Henry's lungs. "You can't—you can't say no."

"Why not?"

"War rules."

Danny turns to leave. Is this really happening? "Your rules," mutters Danny.

Henry watches his friend walk away. "Dinks!"

Pines crowd in on themselves, twisting at the sudden clamor for space, breath. Rough trunks slender to sleek necks spiked with the tough stubs of hacked branches. Henry presses the point of a branch stub with his fingertip: he jerks it back, swiftly composes his bird-boned shoulders, surveys the forest, the trees—every branch a ten-year-old might reach hacked.

For the fire of course.

So he's greedy, Henry thinks. So what?

Greed According to Henry at Ten: to withhold from Henry his rightful destiny. Examples: to withhold from Henry stingray handlebars for his bicycle, a minibike, divinity.

Henry walks forward heel to toe. If Danny were there (he still can't believe Danny had the gall to refuse a mission!) he'd be moving backwards, toe to heel. Back touching back. War rules. Devised, naturally, by Henry. He has two knives, pocketed for now. He follows a dirt path worn smooth by the minibikes of older kids.

Thin grey pines, light brown needles on the growthless ground like a deer's hide. Still, here, in this part of the woods, the yellow sponge of day.

Henry soldiers on.

He enters the Dark Woods where sparks from a sun smoldering

against the treetop mesh spiral to earth, brilliant stricken fighter pilots; where the air is as chilled as the yellow wine Henry's mother drinks at dinner, the ground no longer a needly sponge that gives beneath his sneakers but ashen dirt danced to a resonant floor.

"Shh," says Henry, pretending Danny is by his side. To keep fear at bay.

The log roof of the underground fort has been cracked and caved by older kids who always enter the Dark Woods from the other side, who sift through trees or speed through on minibikes.

"Halt."

Henry imagines that Danny's shoulder blades knock against his own and that Henry does not, in his annoyance, call Danny "Dinks."

Henry says, "Knives out and open," and his calm, unafraid voice creations a pocketknife in each hand.

He smiles. His eyes fire. A lantern, his head swings. His gaze lights a semicircle, illumines the cracked and caved logs, passes, twinges and returns.

Henry has never ventured beyond the underground fort. Beyond it, the Dark Woods pause in a forever dusk.

Henry thinks: my eyes are fire my eyes are fire my eyes…

How to predict which tree conceals an older kid's arm poised to clutch at a ten-year-old's leg? When a minibike will appear in his path, full-throttled, with the suddenness of knives? When indeed. What, you might wonder, possessed Henry to order this frightful hunt for an escapee who believes he's a reaction not a thing; a madman in search of the perfect act that will realize him—him the agent of the event—as divine.

"Run," commands Henry. "Weave."

His arms and legs pump in an off-kilter concert but these thrusting pocketknives, they've lost their shine.

Nothing shines through the morning dusk of the Dark Woods turning now to night which kindles the smoky fires of older kids, and he's seen them during flashlight tag and wondered if, some night, the fires would merge and come licking at his bedroom window— wondered if he'd like that. *Something's happened.* He glances at the blades sticking from his fists, twigs without menace, flames without shine. He leaps a log that lay nearly hidden by pine needles, alerted by a single spike. A lesser creature would have missed this sign.

Flap. His breath catches. Flap. A bird in Henry's chest? He can't budge it. Flap. Its caged wingbeats. A grackle, it must be, the ugliest bird alive. Looks like an oily crow, the second ugliest bird alive. Its droppings turn the ground to a stinking gray sponge, like brain matter.

Henry at Ten: the ground's a bird brain.

He fakes out a hairy net of vines between trees. It's a close call. The net would have snatched him up.

Up. Head up. Watch the trees—the bark. Watch the bark.

This bark that lies like shingles. To glance off this bark is to set the entire forest to jangling like a tambourine, and all the animals will emerge—the grackles dancing down the pines, the grackle inside strutting upwards, pecking. And the older kids, and the madman.

Waiting, Henry thinks, for me to fall.

All creation waiting. All creation watching. Stars extinct for millions of years--their afterlife lights Henry. Not a good time for a bad show. Better to be snatched upward in a hairy net than hurled down into the brain shit of flying monkeys. Humiliated by the bowel movements of grackles. With old madman universe watching. Henry can hardly bear to think for shame.

Shame According to Henry at Ten: the sensation of being forced to dress in hot pink pajamas; punishment for an act that reveals the actor's humanness; morally irrelevant (see vanity); a distraction resulting in strategic, if not fatal, error. Example: a ditch slaps Henry's foot sideways with a sound like…

Punk.

His legs mule-kick over his head, rising as if lifted by vines. The vines snap and Henry whines through the chilled dusk, between lithe bird-necked trees, spike-necked trees, stricken fighter pilot that he is, brilliant in the afterlife's glare.

Knives gone.

He sits, legs sprawled in a slack V. He notices he's wearing shorts.

He can't recall having put them on. And the hole. Since when did he have a hole just above the right knee? He bends at the waist without moving his legs and stares. No blood, whiteness, beautiful because of the hole's depth and the color's purity. Not what he expected. He seems to remember expecting this hole but the purity—few are given the chance to view such a thing. Fewer still to touch. Blessed Henry, he's being tested. What to do?

Into the hole, he dispatches a soiled fingertip that taps on the ivory wall; the wall puckers and Henry jerks his finger back. His leg and shoulders convulse. He swallows vomit. He waits. He raises the finger in front of his face.

Now what, Henry?

He tests wind direction and feels no chill on any side of the anointed fingertip. Deduction: no wind.

Stillness. A heavy cream light, sluiced by branches. The light runs down Henry's hand, coats his arm and filthy legs. He breathes. He's sweetening, becoming pure. Everything is possible now.

Your heavy cream light, Commander.

Henry flexes his shoulders, surveys the purpling hole. It doesn't hurt. A madman lurks—he's not scared. Desire. His bird shoulders twinge. What happened to desire? He must have coughed that out with his wind—it was a rough landing—coughed out a mini-bike, which he wanted more than anything, gray dogs and brown deer, forts of vine-threaded pines, a tough red bike that kickstopped, the handlebars straight not flared not stingray handlebars, which he had pleaded for, stingray handlebars, figuring his chances were good because of the minibike that they wouldn't be so harsh as to refuse both. To his amazement, they did.

He thinks: how could they do that to me?

Something sets the bark of many trees to a quiet jangling, a held high note.

Is this a test? Henry takes it as such.

And decides he's been joking all along. Putting one over on the Dark Woods, he is. If someone were to give him a minibike, he decides, he would take it. Don't be silly, he would be so thankful just to want one again, any one.

He tosses out a small laugh, and hears this: not just any one, Henry. It must be fast. Fast enough to beat your brother's friend Ira's go-cart, which has no governor.

Henry, fireless, blindly eyes the Dark Woods.

"What's a governor?"

He pats the dance floor around him with his palms, strikes something cold and sharp. Spike. He draws it in. Knife. He closes it without checking for blood. What does it matter what got him, spike or knife? Who got him. Maybe it was Henry himself, testing himself, putting one over on his old mad self.

Hell, Henry, everything's possible now.

He slips the knife into the pocket of his shorts, checks to make sure the leghole is still there, the desire, then he glances up.

Here's where one might not believe what happens. One might say, "C'mon, this is the vision of a kid with a hole in his leg, a kid in shock and what's more a kid who thinks so much of himself he could probably will anything he wanted into a moment of being." One might say, "How can one believe what happens when even Henry at age thirty-three alone in a posh pool house in the woods, gasping for salvation from an undying love, might not believe what happens." One might say, "I know he wants to believe but, hey, buddy, don't we all?"

Whatever.

Here's what ten-year-old Henry sees and hears.

Just the other side of the hairy vine net, the madman dances, backpedaling against slowly spreading flames, pausing to peer through the hairnet and smile.

Henry smiles back. He tries to conjure Danny calling his name, Henry, Henry, but it doesn't work this time—Danny is not there— and the grackle in Henry's chest frenzies and does strut upward pecking and singing: *Henry, Henry.*

Knife out and open. Everywhere the scare and the hurt. And the desire. For what, Henry? The entire universe? The madman's fire has punched a hole in the net through which the madman steps backwards. Singed tendrils curl. The madman swivels.

Get up, he says.

Can't.

Grab onto a branch.

No branches. Spikes.

Spike then.

My leg.

Fire's coming.

My eyes.

Fireman's following.

Are fire.

I know.

You know?

My eyes.

Are fire?

Are you.

Fire?

Of me.

Of fire?

You are.

Of you?

You are.

I am?

Your leg.

My leg? My leg's a burning log.

Henry looks down. Blood bastes his skin. He raises his head. The madman, He's smoke, He's thickening approaching mothering whispering I am you are divine—punk.

The Dark Woods howls.

AUGUST 15, 1999
GLAMSHACK

THERE'S a barn behind the Glamshack that used to hold horses. It's small, dark, and dirt-cool inside. It's a long, wooden shed packed these days with recreational equipment owned by the owners of this estate. There's a windsurfing board, a kayak, tennis rackets, and golf clubs and tarps. A plethora of tarps. It's unclear why the tarps. Outside, tall dry grasses rival a wooden rail fence. I sit upon the top rail with late afternoon sun on my bare legs and a view through trees to the road below. It's not much of a view. The oaks grow thick. Cars reveal themselves to me in flashes of light and sound. All comers to the Glamshack must come by this gravel road.

So far I've only seen and heard two cars and definitely no gravel. I've been out here on this fence for a good four hours. My butt's sore. What was the madman trying to tell me in the fire, in the woods? Was he real? Is love? Am I? What am I missing? I jump down from the fence. Peer into the trees.

The trees. The forest. The forest for the trees.

A filter.

I need, I realize, a filter. I need to not stare directly at Her or at me. I need to place this business in a broader body, one through which the greats have moved and insights have arisen and deliverance (yes, deliverance!) has come to pass. I'm so excited to have come upon this notion that I climb and stand on the fence once again, and my exquisite balance in this position gives me a clear view of the road, and I think: Trees. Forests. Seas. The Fruited Plain. Purple Mountain Majesty. Grasses grow like trees, buffalo drift like shining seas, the Indians live so mysteriously and free that it's an insult to the gluttonous horde of white litterbugs spoiling for a fight to the east. It's a provocation. It's…absurd to compare my pathetic love to one of the greatest human tragedies ever. It's criminal, it's wrong.

It's irresistible.

Because my thing for Indians, I'm starting to see, is about a lot more than sprinting through the woods at age ten past a couple fucking—it's about casting my spirit's lot with that of the Tragically Unshackled. I'm also seeing that ever since meeting Her I've harbored the aforementioned hope (aforementioned to Her, on the Lighthouse deck, naked beneath the blanket) that in the course of their war, a tribe, a band, even just one brave managed to light upon a third way, and in the course of tracing their war and (criminally) mine, perhaps I'll discover deliverance.

So I go inside the Glamshack and pick a book off the floor. A book I've read many times. I wrote a letter atop it, a letter to Her, the evening She left for New Orleans. I can still see scrawly indentations in the cover. This book, I recall, is a masterful history of the Plains Indian wars. I open it, flip through, picking, choosing, remembering.

MARCH 27, 1999
HENRY AND CRAZY HORSE

EIGHTEEN FORTY, Independence, Missouri, a wagon train heads west. It's 1848 and California is American. Wyoming in 1851. Ten-thousand Indians show up for a council with the army. Three weeks of dancing and making nice, the sort of behavior, which the army assures will continue so long as the people agree to curb their provocative wandering. South Dakota, 1868. Half the state is promised to the Indians but six years later, Black Hills flash gold. California, 1999. A strong-jawed woman, fierce calves and fighting breasts, lounging in a red bikini on a hot tar roof at noon, says, quite offhandedly, "This guy I date in New Orleans…"

Henry's response: chew his tuna.

They finish their sandwiches and move to Her bed. A king-size imported from Indonesia. On the walls: a painting of a voluptuous mixed-race woman, one breast peeking from a tight dress, lounges on a bed with a pistol beside her thigh; hats and garish feathers and foot-and-a half-long Indonesian penis sheaths made out of bone; a letter Henry does not bother to read.

On the radio: baby-doll rap.

On the dresser: photos of a dude.

Afterward, they lie on their sides, and he strokes Her mane, feet touch feet, toes intertwine, early afternoon sun twinkles through the window they have not bothered to shroud. Kisses. Yes, he still loves kissing Her. Kissing Her ignites lights within Her face. Kissing Her charges his spit with an electric lust and kindles in his chest the perilous burn of tenderness.

"I really like kissing you," he says.

"Is that so surprising?"

"I…guess not," he says, and thinks: Maybe every dude who's ever kissed Her really likes kissing Her. Maybe She expects that, even disdains that. Maybe really liking kissing Her is, in Her eyes, puddling. Maybe the only way not to be a puddler, in Her eyes, is to treat Her like shit.

What is real?

"You said something earlier," says Henry. "About this guy in New Orleans. This guy you dated in New Orleans."

"Date," She corrects, softly and without inflection.

Henry's response: A kiss.

A Mormon cow strays close to an encampment of Indians, and a fool with the name of High Forehead, shoots it, and a braggart named Grattan sets out to arrest the cow killer and, quite offhandedly, brings along a twelve-pound fieldpiece and a mountain Howitzer and somehow things get out of hand, and Grattan gets twenty-four arrows in the skull, and all but one of his men are wiped out and all but one Indian survives, the unfortunate bearing the name of Whirling Bear, a.k.a. Brave Bear, a.k.a. Conquering Bear, a.k.a. Bear that Scatters Enemies, and the Indians hightail it north, and the soldiers are buried in graves so shallow a month later their heads peep at litterbugs, and the press spins the incident into a fiendish Indian plot, and the army vows vengeance, and a man, name of Curly, a.k.a. Crazy Horse, is so unsettled by a premonition of even greater foolishness and savagery to come that he passes three days on a hill without eating and with pebbles between his toes and rocks under his back to ward off sleep, before finally, he sees his horse. With a warrior astride. A warrior with no scalps. With hair below his waist and a pebble behind his ear. Hail spots and lightning streaks adore his form; bullets and arrows shun it. Through a terrible storm and a clutch of outstretched arms, he rides unsullied. And a red-backed hawk circles his head. And…And…And into the irrigated desert east of L.A. flies a man, named You Know Who, who just three days ago learned his beloved "dates" a guy in New Orleans. Into what car dealers bill as the Inland Empire. To attend a wedding of an old college friend. To find in that wide light and mean heat his own medicine.

The ceremony is in the backyard of a ranch-style house. The faith is Baha'i, which Henry has never heard of, and Jewish. The Baha'i officiator looks like a game show host. During the reception, Henry helps others lift the wife up onto a chair, and they dance around with her clumsily. He chats with an ex-girlfriend who is married to a guy Henry doesn't cotton to, clumsily. He chats with two old semi-friends and their wives. He doesn't see what they see in the wives. He feels saddened. He drinks the good keg beer and gets drunk. The sun sets. Toasts at the outdoor tables. Henry has never given a toast in his life, but feels he must say something. He leans toward a semi-friend—a lean and somewhat over-spirited youth whose face is now gray and dessicated—and says, "I'm pining."

A half-hour later, under cover of dancing, he slips away to his rental car, returns to the hotel, checks out, and heads east, beyond irrigation.

He wakes dry-mouthed and sweating in the driver's seat at the entrance to Joshua Tree. Buys a bottle of water and a map that contains a reference to a place called Wonderland. Drives there, gets out and hikes.

It seems that one day, long ago, a localized cloud burst over this place dropping semi-truck-sized boulders on the red earth. Some spread out evenly over the land. Some fell right on top of one another, creating small mountains with chasmed insides. Henry follows a trail until it becomes confining. He climbs, leaping when he must leap great deep gaps. Spidering up cracks, goating ledges. All clumsiness gone. All thoughts on breaking through to…Wonderland. A place tailor-made for him. Broad and bright and arching as a conquistador's helmet. Strewn with the blocks of a frustrated toddler-god. Comprised of tightly married, incomprehensibly huge, slabshapes. In the tightness of the marriages and in the inhuman scale of the marrieds, tension.

And recognition. For this is the very landscape of Henry's childhood inducements of death, days when (nights actually) he would lie in bed and stiffen his body so that a shudder, a squeeze of mercury up a tube, would slip through him and usher in a world where Henry was nothing but consciousness inhabiting a non-world comprised of massive married slabs. Sometimes scary wonky voices materialized, like that of a friend of his who was one year older and always the doctor when they played war with the little sisters. Other times no voices, simply a conscious state of unbeing. As a ten-year-old kid, this state was exciting, and the control Henry had over it, when to enter and exit, dampened the fear.

But around puberty, which for Henry was late, he began to lose control of this state of death. It would visit him at the unlikeliest moments, and his reaction was always the same— nightmare laughter. He would be sitting listening to his English teacher talk about the bond between the boys in *A Separate Peace* and suddenly, he'd be nowhere. And the teacher's voice would go all wonky and Henry must have had an expression come over his face like that of death warmed over because his classmates, those seated nearby, would grin at him, thinking Henry's got some secret on the teacher up his sleeve. And Henry, on account of the absurdity and terror of attention being paid to a dead man, would begin to shake and squeak. Tears would come to his eyes. He'd put his head down, sending the rest of the class into conniptions. Henry laughed silently, befitting a dead person, but his classmates eventually busted forth with guffaws, and these, along with the teacher's increasingly strained voice, wonked around the room as if each person had his own distortionist bullhorn and their images, through the tears, blurred and their noses and eyes shifted positions in unnatural ways.

If daytime dying was absurd, night offered up forms to fill the void. He'd lie in his bed in a ball on the pillow, back against the wall, watching the doorway. No normal scaredy-cat, he'd be wishing for a man with a gun to appear. Something of substance to dissipate the vampires and werewolves and man-eating sludge. Things got bad enough that finally Henry went to his father and confessed. A good and kind man, his dad consulted a psychologist, who said it was due to the turbulence of puberty and would subside when— to paraphrase the eminent professional—the hair around Henry's dick was all grown in. This seemed to satisfy his father, but it did Henry no good. How can dickhair stave off werewolves? No, what Henry needed was a force as fierce as death. As enchanting as a demon. Stories of a vengeful God who occasionally, arbitrarily, wreaked mercy. Superstitions handed down from generations that continued to hamper his family's progress in the modern world. Make-out sessions at the dinner table between mom and dad. And he wasn't going to get it from his loving, supportive family. The ritual of watching their son eat broccoli like a giant eats trees was as close to worship as Henry's family got. After relating the psychologist's finding, Henry's stumped father said, "I can understand if something happened here, but nothing has."

Wonderland. The fearsome recognition spurs Henry on to feats of alpinism. Shirtless, lean and gleaming, he yearns higher, finds a crack, and follows it up. Summits on a punch bowl filled with water. Prays to it then lifts his face to the sky and prays to that. He fears nothing in this place of nothing because every chasmed mountain, every tense marriage, speaks now, for the first time, of one thing— one exultant Happening: Her.

Henry on the mountaintop: "God," he says, as if he said it all the time and not just when he was scared or wanted something. "I love…"

Crazy Horse throws a feast in honor of his one true love, Black Buffalo Woman, a mother of three who is married to No Water (or

No Face), and she expresses her appreciation by depositing the kids with relatives, saying sayonara to No Face and shacking up with her one true love, Crazy Horse, and while Sioux custom is fine with this divine realignment, No Face is not; he bursts in on the newlyweds and shoots Crazy Horse. With a bullet buried beneath his left nostril, Crazy Horse falls into the fire, badly wounded but miraculously destined for a full recovery. Given that No Face is known as a violent and jealous man, this sort of behavior might have been anticipated by anyone but Crazy Horse, who, like Henry, is a man whose eyes, in the words of our author, Evan S. Connell, "looked beyond things."

He helps Her tend the garden in her ten-by-ten-foot front yard. She has enclosed it in a knee-high white wire fence. She takes him by the hand and tells him the names of things. Agapanthus is the only one that sticks and only because it sounds like panther and panther makes him think of Her. They do this in late spring evenings, light like yellow wine. In the house's other unit lives a family, a father about Henry's age who looks much older, a mother and two small children, boy and girl. The three-year-old boy constantly wears a towel for a Superman cape, and the girl, who is five, is smart and pretty. They stand around watching Henry and Her garden and sometimes She lets them use the hose. The father, a heroin addict and construction worker, comes outside with a beer, sits on the steps and says, "How are things, Miss Thing." Miss Thing because there are no known words or phrases to describe a creature of Her gut-level seductive-ness. She doesn't answer, She's bent over a plant, Her hair hanging stringy, Her hands grubby and veined, and Henry can't help staring at his animal, his innocent, his creepy crawly Miss Thing. For right now, in the plants, She stands stripped of affect. She stands pure. And pure, for Her, is…entirely physical. Is to be entirely inhabited by physical sensation and all its possible nuances. Of flower and leaf. Fish and deer. A hard and slick rhythm. Pure, for Her, is to be enchanted. And, in turn, to enchant.

Henry accepts a beer from the father and joins him on the step.

The children have taken the hose. They squirt each other, shrieking. She says, from Her stance in the plants, "Henry, come here," and of course he does. He crouches with Her, and She peels back a terribly fragile petal, rests it, without picking it, on Her thumb, and says, "Only three days a year this blooms. These three. We're in it. Isn't it absolutely beautiful? Next year, promise me, you'll visit them." She turns to the father. "What's the date today?"

A moment after She says, "you'll visit them," Henry hears, creak, and "you'll" becomes "we'll," and there in the petal is a vision of the future, of one year hence, of Henry and Her returning from a cabin in Georgia, or a thatched hut in Bangladesh, hand in hand and calm as the dew, the second annual pilgrimage to the three-day bloom, and that moment between "you'll visit them" and *creak*, it feels like it never happened.

They make love in the afternoon and go for walks up curving streets rife with plants. Holding hands, an act that affects Henry more than fucking. She takes his palm for moments at a stretch, gracefully withdraws, and he can feel the chilled wind on his knuckles. Minutes later, repeat. The effect, on Henry, is a constant yearning. He tries not to clutch at Her, but then he sees a small white house built to resemble a Mexican bungalow and it's demure behind a frolic of plants pulsing like coals. He clutches Her hand, draws Her to him, says, "God, let's go to Mexico."

They plan a languorous dinner at a nearby French restaurant. First drinks at the round outdoor tables, the air thick with bougainvillea, then dinner by the fireplace inside. The lodge holds precious few patrons. Henry, a shoveler of meals, takes his time. Wine. She in a clingy, yellow and black dress with a slit up to high-thigh. It is his birthday and She has bought him things. Irises, his favorite. He's never received flowers from a woman. A necklace, which, if it came from anyone else, he would never consider wearing. He dons it and feels pretty. A short-sleeve shirt with buttons and a wide collar, something a Costa Rican might wear, something Henry would never wear. But he takes off his t-shirt and buttons it on. Henry the jewelry-wearing Costa Rican. Embarrassing and thrilling.

"You know how I chose these things?"

"They challenge me."

She nods. He leans over the table and they kiss.

"I love how you challenge me. I really…love it. I hope I do something similar for you."

"You do."

"We share the burden of discovery."

"We do."

Venison arrives, a graceful meat. She cuts a piece, shifts the fork to Her right hand, a move that endears Her to him. Henry watches Her chew and feels close to exploding. Far more satisfying to feel Her eat than actually eat himself. As if he were only able to experience these sensations, these subtleties of taste, through Her.

As if, in this rarified air of love, he is Her.

As if the poor sap can no longer feed himself.

He cuts his meat European style.

They talk of Her travels through Indonesia, sleeping in stilt houses with entire families, circumventing the law to explore territories off-limits to foreigners, poling up a river with a massive musclebound native named Stallones who She "definitely would have fooled around with." Fooled, Henry thinks, or fool? And he has the feeling he's asked this question before. And then he remembers. This guy in New Orleans you dated? he asked Her once. And She answered, Date, soft and without inflection. Just like now. Which should get him thinking, but it does not. He does not ask himself what it means for Her to decide to make love, or to not? He does not ask because he wants to believe that sex, for Her, is profound. And particular. Which it is for him. He's scared, Henry. But more than that, he's captured by the rarified air of the evening, an air that, he believes, speaks of love.

They talk of Her straight A's in physics, which She does not study now, and he holds forth on jobs he's had—ranch hand in Wyoming, handyman in Utah, pot grower in Oregon (how many times, he asks himself, these tired stories, how many times?) and mountains he's scaled, deserts across whose vivid sands he's greatly planed. Of travel and adventure they do speak and not a word, not a thought of the mind and motivation of the torturer, of New Orleans.

She sets Her fork and knife on Her plate. The fire, though it's nearly summer, intones. Tile floor and heavy wooden tables. Henry and She sit in an alcove, overlooking, medieval. The Bee Queen and Her Latin Prince. She lays a tiny card on the table. "When we move," it says in Her handwriting, "we travel."

Hiding a sob, Henry sips red wine. Swallows. Says, "You know you told me you don't know who you are?'

"I don't."

"I don't believe you. I think maybe at one time that was true. I think you hide behind that now. I think it makes things easier for you."

She smiles. "You got me."

Later, at Her house, when Henry emerges from her bathroom, he finds Her kneeling on the couch, facing the back wearing heels and a corset. His mood is soft, swoony love, but he forces the shift and performs.

The next day, he buys his first plant. A drasina from the local hardware store that only needs water once a week. And calls Her with the news.

"I'm seeing a guy who's never owned a plant."

"I now own a plant," he says, looking at it proudly.

She says, "I'm going to New Orleans. For a visit. I'll call you in a week."

I'll call you in a week. Soft and without inflection. Like "fool" or "date". As if the Lighthouse and the Love Nest inhabit separate universes, and are therefore compatible, or at least not incompatible. In desperation he even tries to grasp this, that they are not incompatible. And nearly dies trying. And the days that follow Her departure reek like burning oil. The nights are nightmare laughter. The plant is murderous. To escape it, he credit-cards a flight to the Midwest, to the sexy hearth of a woman named Sally, a woman for whom he once played Lord Byron and thought he meant it.

"You may think people care what you're doing, that people are watching, but guess what? Nobody's fucking watching."

He says this standing in Sally's kitchen. His flight arrived less than an hour ago. Behind the house is a screened-in porch, and behind that grass sloping to a dock, a lake. It's night. There's a wall hanging she crocheted herself. He says his piece and then, without another wasted word, walks out the back porch down to the dock and gazes up, searching for the Pleiades, anticipating the thin snap of the screen door and the dot dot dot of her feet on the steps, the mothering sound of rain on a roof. It used to be their constellation, the Pleiades. After some difficulty, he finds it. No snap and no dot and no snap and no dot. Snap. An elegant hand like wind through his hair. Or rather, wind through his hair like an uncaring hand. The world is murdering him. For the first time ever, he actually looks at the Pleiades rather than imagining someone else watching him—or better yet imagining someone else watching him and his beloved— look at it. Cold things, stars, even Seven Sisters huddled together for warmth in deep space. What of their light? Quite possible the Pleiades died millions of years ago and he's receiving severed, lifeless energy, like a leg in the mail. He feels depraved. He sees his face, and hands touching his face without affection. Great Lake waves embrace the dock's pylons, over and over, simulated intimacy without end. "Whores!" he says out loud. A night fisherman's boatlight winks green. Green the color of light's essence. He once described as such, in a rare unwatched moment, a leaf backlit by the sun. Now he understands that green is the color of absolute absence. Beneath him, boats lashed together wheeze like asthmatics. His presence is sensed by bats. *Screech.* He could be anything big and warm. He understands this too now. The severed limbs of the Seven Sisters grapple for a grip on this fine figure of an invisible man. He turns toward the house, its green-apple glow, its brown-seeded core. Lovely pure fruit save—

And she...rises on tiptoes. To find him, his form in the dark. To discover him anew. To help birth a beautiful creature from this terror. To take down the wall hanging. To take up implements— long, fat needles. To disappear into an easy chair. To crochet.

Wait!

She stands! She moves to the screen door. She catches sight of him on the dock and waves her arms like someone official guiding a jetliner to the gate. The needles, one in each hand, flash.

"Hey, Henry," she says. "C'mon inside. You'll get eaten alive."

The desired choreography, which describes a scenario of pursuit followed by discovery culminating in the gathering up of Henry the Princely Foundling in the arms of Sexy Sally, is stymied by the implements. How can she open the screen door with an implement in each hand? What's more, dignity precludes him from calling out with instructions like, *Hey, shift your implements!* But then she does it—she shifts the implement from her left hand into her right, which now holds two, and with her elegant left, she unlatches the screen door and pushes through and spatters down the steps and glides toward him with her plain white t-shirt and little blue cutoffs and camel colored ankle-length cardigan flowing out behind like angel wings and stops a foot from him, studying his face with a look of bemusement.

She says, "Am I right so far?"

Henry cocks his head, suddenly wary.

"I went looking for you, I found you, I came for you. That right so far?"

This is not the desired choreography.

"Shall we embrace now?" she says.

A mosquito whines in Henry's ear. With her free hand, Sally slaps at her arm.

"Damn," she says. "How about we do the next part inside?"

And she smiles, in that same sickening bemused fashion, and Henry raises his gaze to meet hers and yes she is beautiful and no question she could have a fleet of 747's at her gate just by lifting her implements and Lord wouldn't it be lovely to taxi on in there and after all isn't this what he's been waiting for out on this chilly dock with the lifeless limbs of stars and the green of absence and the screech of bloodsuckers and the whores and fish and yet not only has the choreography gone wrong on the outside, it's defective on the in, and (with a nauseating gut-flip) Henry realizes the entire script must be ditched, that he can't progress to the embrace no matter where it occurs because, for the first time in his life, he can't mix and match lovelies, there's only one right gate for him now and it's guarded by thieves and whores.

Henry's response? Catch the next flight to the Coast.

Black Buffalo Woman and Crazy Horse separate—a tragedy whose details are mercifully lost to time—and into Crazy Horse's lodge walks Black Shawl, who he does not love but with whom he conceives a daughter, who he loves dearly, and when she dies of cholera, he climbs her burial scaffold and after three days up there nestled beside her tiny body, he descends and engages in a lot of cold lone wandering far beyond the warmth and protection of his village, during which time a lot of white miners turn up dead in the Black Hills, scalps intact, a single arrow driven into the ground beside each corpse, and when asked about this unseasonable behavior, Crazy Horse speaks of holes where he sleeps, spirits whose assistance he's securing, plans he's concocting.

These mad plans.

Not twenty-four hours after his departure, he's back in the Lighthouse.

Four days after Her departure She calls. He is in the Lighthouse drinking fat cans of beer with a friend. Pacing in socks so as not to disturb the downstairs neighbors—Henry hates leaving traces, craves something in this world that bears his mark. They chat, She and he. At some point, he realizes She's working up to something, later still, realizes what it is and offers to pick Her up at the airport. She accepts, says, "I've got to go now, we just put in a video."

We. Soft and without inflection. It flaps like a bat throughout the Lighthouse. It's so clear he can see the hairs on its wings, so close he could reach out and grab it. But he doesn't. He sits in fear of this creature for whom nothing is incompatible. For whom everything is possible. It is part of Her power, this absolute freedom to act as She pleases. And it paralyzes Henry, makes him ashamed, and aroused, and all he can do is sit there, sucking silence.

"You've gone away," She says.

"Yes." Then. "I'll be there."

In the airport, he goes to kiss Her and She gives him Her cheek. In his car, he tries again and She permits lips. In Her bed, they make love and She cries. In the morning, they drive south to a regal old university in a hot dry valley where She is considering attending yet another grad school, the exact nature of which is unclear. A student gives them a tour. In the parapet of the Spanish-style bell tower Henry climbs the metal mesh meant to discourage suicide attempts. When he returns to Her, She is asking the student about jobs in law in the area. Henry is beside Her and She knows this and he knows the fiancé is in law school.

They are striding onto a wide, warm lawn.

"Why did you ask about law jobs?"

"Henry, you know he's moving out here."

"You're shameless."

"You knew."

"To a stranger, in front of me, you ask these questions like they're nothing."

"Henry."

"If he steps foot in this state," Henry says, "you'll never see me again."

They stop in the middle of the lawn, lower themselves. University life surrounds them, bicycles, grass sleepers, head-down walkers, and high-pitched talkers.

"He's my enemy."

"Don't say that."

"It's the nature of things."

"I hate that."

"If he moves here, you'll be my enemy too."

They wrangle until both are exhausted, standing now, embracing for God knows how long. A moment. Outside the car, they make out furiously.

Henry: "I'd like to do indecent things to you."

Her: "I'd like you to do them."

They drive even further south, through redwoods, environs which Henry will soon inhabit though he doesn't know it, and She says that maybe the fiancé will be history after all. She says, "He said to me, 'We were the same for a long time and now you're moving ahead of me.' And it's true. And he's going to be tied to a job, and I need someone who can travel."

"We can travel."

"Yes."

Down a winding dark road opening onto a beach town where they secure a motel with a pool, She wants a pool, and they make love, She's on Her back on the bed and Her torso hangs off, Her palms on the floor, She's screaming "Oh God Oh Fuck!" Her breasts are feverpink Her hardhoney legs slap the sheets Her pussy seeps Her jaw to the sky and Henry fucks Her, it is he who is fucking Her, he who runs the gloriously indecent show.

To a bar with a pool table that takes quarters. Henry goes to the bartender for quarters and passes a man with massive muscular arms and a polo shirt who asks him if he's "playing on that table." Of course he's playing on that table. Henry's woman's standing by it and he's going to the bar for quarters. When he gets back, the man is racking the balls, She chalking Her stick.

"What the fuck, man," says Henry, gauging the biceps, thinking, fuck, I'm going to have to go up against them. "I told you I was just going for quarters.

"I didn't know," says the man, but his look says 'Try it.'

"Fuck you didn't." Biceps or no, Henry is ready.

"It was me," She says. "I told him he could play."

Henry backs against the wall, a stake through his throat. She asks his advice during the game, implying teamness, and he says, "It's your game. You play it."

"He ain't giving up nothing," says the man.

All is symbolic, Henry knows this in his gut. And then—creak —he forgets.

In bed, She berates him and he apologizes and in the morning they fuck like creatures bred for sex and She swims in the pool while he lounges deckside, watching and later, on the beach, they dash through the receding cycle of waves and are too late. They get drenched, step through a rock with a hole in it to a tiny cove beneath cliffs and She is naked, he touches Her purple nipple, She says stop he says why She says cause it's working. Above them, on the cliffs, tourists. They dash back through the hole, through the waves, watch a ropey old man with dreadlocks dance to hippie drums. They buy Henry a used Converse All-Star t-shirt and Her a new silk dress under which She wears nothing, yanking stares from men and women (Lord how She loves those stares). But It doesn't matter where they go now. It doesn't matter what they do. They could go and do anything and the experience would be the same—fevered bliss.

Everything is possible.

AUGUST 15, 1999
GLAMSHACK

I'M STANDING waist high in crisp grass. When did I descend from the fence? When did I return to the fence? From whence this night? I walk and grasses tick softly against my legs and shatter. Funny how the evening has brought no dew. Yet. I circle around the barn to the back of my house where wood too green to burn is stacked. Out front, I mount the porch. My hand's on the handle of the screen door and I pause, turn. The thought of going inside, drinking a glass of water, reading, undressing—the thought of doing these living things makes it hard to breathe, and I think of Crazy Horse and massacres and muscle-bound dudes shooting pool and sex. Which of these thoughts will cast Her in the darkest light, will help me get free?

Only problem is I see now that She let him rack the balls and chalk his cue because She was scared. It wasn't a betrayal of me, as I thought then, as I so want to believe now; it was a simple fearful response to superior strength. And when I called Her on it, in my pouty wounded way, She owned up. Courageously. At the cost of Her own standing in my eyes. *It was me*, She said. *I told him he could play.* God, why did She have to own up?

What about sex?

Lots of sex.

Lots of profound sex. Profound for me and for Her. I see this now too. I see also that what makes our sex profound is that it's particular to us alone—that it's Her and only Her I'm fucking, that it's me Her egg-shaped thrusts rise mightily to meet. And then into this truth's fragrant garden steps an oily suspicion: while the sex may be profound for both of us, it's particular only to me. Which makes no sense. How can sex be profound and not particular? Does that mean She could have profound sex with anyone? Billions of dudes out there, all potential profound-sex partners? I suspect not. I suspect I'm missing something. What? Is the thing I'm missing contained in that terrifying and thrilling notion that everything is possible? When did I first hear the phrase everything is possible? With Her? With the madman?

The madman.

In the presence of the madman—if there ever was a madman—I was paralyzed with fear and smitten with desire, for I heard, or felt, that everything was possible. And that's exactly what happened with thirty-three-year-old me and Her. Paralyzed and smitten in the presence of the one for whom nothing is incompatible. For whom everything is possible. In the presence of the one for whom everything is possible, a man becomes big as the sun. And then, with a word, soft and without inflection, he's nothing. And nothing is divine. And I can't bear the notion, that they are the same, Her and him; I can't live if nothing is divine. Must everything is possible mean everything is divine therefore nothing is? Can't there be another interpretation? Please?

JUNE 7, 1976
HENRY AND THE MADMAN

HENRY AT TEN, lying in the guest bed, in which his grandmother sleeps when she visits. He's got sixteen stitches in his leg, sewn fresh that afternoon. He's laboring under an eerie smell. He's thinking: divinity.

Henry thinks he knows enough about what divinity means to know it makes Henry bigger, stronger, quicker. Though he isn't big, he is strong for his size and many a twelve-year-old has been pinned face down with his arm wrenched behind his back and ordered to eat onion grass because he judged Henry ripe for a showoff wrestle. Many a startled thirteen-year-old has tumbled short of the end zone because he judged Henry a weak tackler. And Henry is fast; he is known for that. No one is fool enough to challenge Henry on speed.

So Henry is. He's…

Laboring under a smell that's turned terrifying. A smell beyond burning pines. This smell has to do with the nature of the Dark Woods, the scent of oil and metal, the vertigo following loss of desire, the burndown of daylight to dusk and aloneness, the anticipation of ignition. Possibility, like a grackle, frenzies, and the madman is dancing so rapt that Henry, watching, might as well be alone but then the madman (also referred to as the fireman) swivels and smiles and addresses Henry, and the fireman and the madman is…a scary older kid who's ditched his minibike behind a tree. Who's playing in the woods with Roman candles and bottle rockets, which are wrong because his mother says so. Who's fire's gone wild.

Henry is bleeding in his grandmother's bed. Bleeding and shivering and sweating. Say it's still so: Danny is my best friend Danny is my best friend Danny mommy all I ever want is a minibike mommy do you know, mommy, what He said to me?

Dot dot. The sound of his mother's footsteps. Dot. Moving toward his room. In the tone of her step, he knows she holds his dinner on a metal tray. Then he smells the food. It wrestles with the Dark Woods. It's a mommysmell and Henry cleaves to it.

Henry's mother walks into the room. She lays the tray of food on the sick table over his midsection. She bends toward his gauze-wrapped leg.

Henry's sutured skin tingles. "Mom?"

"Dear?"

"What's divine?"

Henry's mother straightens, turns toward her son. It's then he notices, through the window, the green-black bloat of the air, the absence of birdsong that normally at this hour on a summer evening drills the sky with sound in the same way the stars will soon with light; the absolute silence, in fact, within which howls the Dark Woods with a sound that is a smell, a smell so strong it eats the mommysmell and there is no more mommysmell ever again and was there ever a mommysmell? Was there ever really only one smell and Henry's younger-kid self made-believe there was a mommysmell because he was scared and he was small and those days are gone, now, after what happened in the Dark Woods today. Henry thinks in his grandmother's bed, mommy smells like the Dark Woods.

Her smile is terrifying.

Henry, pinned beneath the sick table, smiles back.

"You dear," Henry's mother says. "You are what's divine."

Eight minutes later, which Henry tallies on his grandmother's wind-up alarm clock, Henry hears his family sitting down to dinner. He glances out the window. The air is grotesque, but it's all there is now, and he must go to it, he must find in it something to hold onto like he held onto the mommysmell. A long time ago. When Henry was a child.

Gently, he slides the sick table off his midsection. He stands and, a nimble cripple, crawls easily through the window. At the shed, he stops for a weapon, chooses a shovel because it's sharp and doubles as a fire-fighting tool. Walking with it on the road, he thinks of his mother's answer to his question of what's divine. It's far too much and not nearly enough. Before today, divinity meant bigger, faster, stronger. Now he knows it means something else, but his parents, good people, have never brought it up. Did she mean only he is divine? And if only he, God, there's…

Only me.

He changes his grip on the shovel, one-handed to two.

He's out there. He must be. What if he is?

Shovel out and ready. For everything that is possible now.

He passes the neighbor girls jumping rope.

"Where are you going Henry?" one says.

"With your leg," says the other.

"Your stitches."

"That shovel."

"I'm going," says Henry.

Into the woods.

AUGUST 16, 1999
GLAMSHACK

I'M RUNNING fire trails through the woods and I'm lost. And strong. I feel I can run faster and farther than anyone who might care to match me. I remember when this feeling was my only notion of divinity and I wonder: what is my notion now? What's beyond nothing?

Round the rim of a ravine, there are no leaves on the fire trail but below, they clog the ravine like newspaper wadded in a woodstove. The air is dry and cool on account of the redwoods and dark though it's only morning. Dark like the Dark Woods that ate my mother's smell, the mommysmell that thrilled me and terrified me. I'm lost, lost in the woods but my stride is a lope, and I can feel my shoulders muscle every time my arms pump, and I realize I've been running lost ever since I lost my mother's smell and climbed out the window with my stitches and my desire and my fear and went into the woods searching for the madman and my breath now is piston-driven and I'm so tall my mind touches…madness.

Is madness what's beyond nothing? Is madness what's divine? Is everything possible for me too? Are we all three finally the same—Him and Her and Me?

These fire trails, they're so smooth it's like running on water. Running up water.

To a lake, a brokedown dock, a meadow, blond grass stiff in this windless heat. It strikes me, this hillside where I run, where I live, is awaiting conflagration. Cloudless heat neverending. Madness ascending. Fire impending. Jaw pore tit blending and love, love, love is everything love is nothing love is…

Love is a hangnail.

APRIL 17, 1999
LOVE IS A HANGNAIL

HENRY DOES not, typically, walk into big buildings; he walks between them. And if he does get the chance to walk into one, it's usually by some workman's entrance in the back reached by a foul-smelling concrete walkway between the building and a sewage canal, and then, when he reaches the door, it is red and rusty and heavy and must be pushed on hard, and when it gives, it gives onto a phlegm-floored kitchen and the staff eyes him as he makes his way across the moldy linoleum, between steel bowls and massive black griddles spitting bacon fat and once in a while, some omelet juggler calls out, "Hey, asshole, where's your hairnet?" Then, as likely as not, Henry's hand will smoketrail to his head.

But something's happened to Henry. These days, he walks right through the gleaming brass revolving doors.

Love's happened, yes. And the woman he's in love with appears to know about moments, that they should be entered wide-eyed and bare-headed, lingered in, permitted to become complete and once complete, cherished as begottens.

But more than love or watching or moments, what's happened to Henry is war. How it began seems as irrelevant to him now as the question of whether he should continue to fight. Of course he'll continue to fight. Survival orders it. Desire blows a thousand horns. Dreams unfurl the banners of a new world where all cheeks are sunblushed, all fingers interlaced, all moments magic. This new world is just behind the enemy line, only a hundred yards or so away, and that line is manned by *only one man*. The fact that the man is Her fiancé doesn't move Henry in the least. The man is the enemy, and a pathetic one at that. Henry, so Henry reasons, is better. He supports this reasoning with a conceptual mangling of something the Conquistador said about the natural order of the universe. As Henry reasons it the natural order of the universe decrees that Henry take this woman as his own. Give him enough time—and he's only got about three more weeks until She travels back to New Orleans for the summer—and he will have logged enough magic moments with Her to win.

Behind Henry, the brass doors revolve with a sound like, hush, hush, hush. He strides across the marble-tiled lobby to the reception counter and says, "Raynard."

"You mean Raynard Productions?" says the guard.

"Sure," says Henry, smiling indulgently. "Raynard Productions."

"Seventh floor. Suite 702."

In the elevator, a wood-paneled affair, a cute young woman, probably a production assistant just out of college, wearing stockings—in Henry's world, they are a rare and erotic sight—smiles at him. Three men, a few years her senior, a few years Henry's junior, wearing sweater vests and new work boots, discuss food photography. Henry calmly watches the numbers rise.

At Suite 702, he opens the door without knocking, enters a vast chamber, a warehouse space meant to conjure Roman Ruin. Thin blocks of pale stone comprise the floor. On the near wall, a winged god in stone relief, one wing busted off. Chipped stone pillars. A kitchenette with blood-red counters. Through man-sized windows bright spades of sun enter, turning up mysterious etchings in floor stones and a goddess in an open sport coat lounging against a pillar, clenching a string of pearls in her tiny teeth.

A substantial breast steals out.

"Sexy," says Raynard, clicking his camera. "Sex-Eee."

Her hands reach back and clasp the pillar.

Both breasts steal out.

"Fuck. Fuck. Yes. Fuck." A thousand and one clicks. "Hair! I need hair!"

A woman is conjured from an unexcavated corner of the chamber. She rushes the Goddess and tosses her hair like a salad. The Goddess looks straight at Henry.

Henry's thoughts: Hair! I need hair! Hair! I need hair! Hair! I need…

On and on, like an ambulance siren. So stricken is our warrior by this lettuce-topped deity that all he can do is send out this mute SOS. *Hair I need hair!* The smile from the elevator girl didn't elicit such a reaction. Nor did the glances from the sweater-vested food photogs. Those, Henry simply slid into his quiver, received as the conqueror's due. But this woman, with the steal of a breast and a quick, direct look, she's turned the universe upside down, threatened to invalidate his war and with that his entire reason for being. With a subtle tonal shift, the ambulance wail clarifies. *Her I need Her!*

The stylist withdraws, the hair appears unchanged, and the Goddess assumes a more demure position—head bowed, arms crossed in front of her, breasts concealed. A thousand and one clicks. Henry slides behind a pillar. He spies a table in the kitchenette laden with pastries and wine and fruit, focuses on a mango, and imagines Her—not Salad Lady—eating it. Tries to conjure the sensations though he's never eaten a mango, and gets the taste of a crabapple. Still, he manages to evoke the brutal jaw, which is enough, for now, to quiet the siren.

He sidles around the pillar to find Raynard, the Goddess and the stylist striding toward him. He braces himself.

"Henry, right?" says Raynard.

"Mr. Raynard."

"You've been hiding."

"I didn't want to disturb the, uh, process."

"Isn't that what you're here to observe? The process?"

"Observe, yes," says Henry, gaining his legs, "but not alter."

"A professional," says Raynard.

The Goddess and the stylist move to the table, standing over it. The stylist begins peeling a mango. The Goddess pours herself a liberal glass of red wine, drinks deeply. On her honed cheeks, a blush stirs. A sunspade catches her bare calf. She whispers something to the stylist and they giggle. The stylist, a bony woman with blue streaks in her hair, large black glasses and painfully bitten fingernails, tongues mango juice from her lower lip and smiles pleasantly at Henry.

"New to fashion?" asks the stylist.

"What?" says Henry.

"You seem a little, uh…"

"I'm not."

"Good."

"New to fashion."

"Too bad."

"Why too bad?"

The stylist glances at Raynard. She turns back to Henry, still with her pleasant smile. "Such a fucked-up business."

"Wine?" says the Goddess, lifting her glass toward the men. She's got an eye cocked at the stylist. Behind her, sun strikes; the one-winged deity lights up.

Raynard shakes his head. He walks to the table and breaks off a grape, which he does not eat.

Henry joins the crew. He doesn't trust himself with either fruit or wine. Nothing giving or wet. His muscles feel like splints on his skeleton, a far cry from fighting armor, but better hard than soft. "I've got a cold."

"Go on," says Raynard. "Profiling a fashion photographer for a glamour magazine can't be that important to you."

"Fruit?" says the stylist, raising a green pear in a twiggy hand.

The Goddess has got the rim of her glass resting against her upper lip, elbows together, jacket parted enough/not enough, and she is studying Henry with narrowed green eyes.

Wine, she mouths, like a command.

"Wine," says Henry. "Sure, yeah, I'll have a glass. What the hell."

The Goddess and the stylist smile, Raynard shakes his head. Something is transpiring, Henry realizes, and he's been pegged either as a god or a fool or an idle toy.

The Goddess pours a glass of red, twists the bottle at the last moment, hands Henry his wine. "Here you are…Henry?"

"Henry." Accepting the glass. "Yes. Yes and…"

"You're not interested in us. You're here for the great and powerful Raynard."

The stylist squints through her glasses at Henry. "Run," she says huskily.

Henry does not run. He drinks, and wills himself in Wonderland, on the mountaintop. *God, I love…Her I need Her…*

"Henry." Wonky and nightmarish. "How's Roland."

"Who?"

"Your boss."

"Oh," says Henry, setting his wine on the table, realizing Raynard's referring to the Conquistador. "Good, he's good."

"He's a bit crude for some, but me, I like him."

"So do I."

"I like a man with a past. Refreshing for the likes of me. I spend my days with twenty-something models."

The Goddess and the stylist have retired to the far corner of the chamber, a dark triangle guarded by an arc of sun. They face one another on stools, heads bowed. The Goddess drinks.

"He doesn't talk much about it his past," says Henry.

"Wouldn't expect him to," says Raynard. "Bit of a tragedy. He was a comer." Raynard rolls the grape between his thumb and forefinger.

Henry studies him, thinks: I hate this job. Glances at the siren in the corner and vaults to the safety of the mountaintop: God, I love…

"So," says Raynard, "what do you want to know about me besides the fact that I'm rich and not handsome and models fuck me on a regular basis because they think I can get them work?"

Henry looks at his legal pad. "Grip," it says. "Gaffer." The words surrounded by paper-piercing doodles. He flips over the page. "Make hay hay hay hay hay hay hay hay hay fuck you if you don't make hay hay." Flips the page again. "Gorgeous." Sees the snake-like belly, the purple nipples, the agapanthus on Her street, the purity of Her in plants. Sees vividly now the land he's fighting for and looks up. He's swathed in a sudden calm.

"Gorgeous," says Henry. "Please define 'gorgeous' for me, Mr. Raynard."

A thousand and one clicks. A cry from Raynard, a rush by the stylist and a salad toss. The Goddess bows her head, eyes sideways. "Yes. Fuck." Head flung back against the pillar. Mouth open revealing filed teeth. Down to a squat, palms on the stone floor, a calf bulges and the pearlstring swings and the jacket parts and once again the Goddess looks right at—.

Me.

Fuck.

Henry takes notes. "Head back against pillar. Lips part. Squatting pearls. Squatting pearls. I love…"

He does not look up again until the thousand-and-first click. The sun has settled elsewhere in the city. The bay, through the window, is dark and flat. Raynard is putting away his camera equipment. The stylist, like a child with blocks and holes of various shapes, fits paints and implements into their slots. The Goddess walks toward Henry, and he begins writing in his notebook. "Head. Squat." He flips toward the front, to the fruits of the interview he just completed. "A hangnail." Raynard's definition of gorgeous. The Goddess passes Henry without a glance.

A hangnail.

"A hangnail," Raynard explained during the interview. "Let me put it this way: Models are models because they have distinctive features. Sometimes exaggerated features. Features that, in print in particular, can be easily disassembled from the rest. The result is the isolation of single features. Cheekbone. Nose. Tit. Draw out the otherness of these things and cheekbone falls off cheekbone, nose from nose, tit from tit. What you're left with is a noncontextual, de-named object, a distinctive, exaggerated no-named thing. Nothing, if you will, which is also everything and stirs in the viewer a mystical sensation of peering through an open door into the cosmos."

"A jaw," Henry said, "could become a door to the entire universe."

"Exactly."

"Pores."

"One pore, all you need."

"Any jaw? Any pore? If you isolate anything, will anything become a door to anyone?"

"Absolutely."

"So the feeling someone in love gets when they look at the one they love, or some part of the one they love, anyone could get that feeling if they looked at it right. Anyone could be the one you love."

"Anyone."

"So you've cracked the mystery."

"I never contended I was a visionary."

"No."

"A humble craftsman, me."

"Full of shit," Henry said under his breath.

"What?"

"You're full of shit."

"Ah, a deft interviewer."

"Is that a joke?"

"Do you like jokes?"

"I hate monsters. I just fucking hate monsters."

Even Raynard is left comebackless; he stands rigid, then reaches out to touch a pillar, sniffs. The Goddess and the stylist, safe behind their arc of sun, peer toward the two men. And Henry is terrified. The great and powerful Raynard has just thrust him into the dead place, the place of intermarried slabshapes, the pre-pube realm of werewolves and evil muck—Wonderland before the War. The Goddess's sun arc becomes a witchy ring of fire. Raynard is a pale zombie, and the Roman ruin decor speaks of satanic ritual.

From down deep, Henry can feel the fizz of nightmare laughter. He can also hear the Conquistador's voice: "No shit, you're a pussy."

You're a man, Henry tells himself. You're a man.

"I wasn't talking about you," Henry says. Wonky and nightmarelike. Laughter threatening.

"What a relief," says Raynard.

"I think you're scaring me."

"You scare easy."

"No, hard."

"What are you scared of—ah, listen to me. You're the interviewer and here I am playing the shrink."

Raynard lifts his hand from the pillar, crosses his arms. The Goddess and the stylist, like nymphs in the wood, bend to one another once again.

"I was talking about a world where nothing's real except you," Henry says.

"Me?" says Raynard.

"You. Me. Anyone."

"I see."

"Where nothing except you is divine."

Raynard nods, as if he understands.

"A world like that," says Henry, "is full of monsters."

Henry glances around this fake Roman ruin. Gray stone dusklight. On the table, beside the bottle of red, yellow wine like his mother used to drink at dinner. Raynard himself a lightless, granite-colored emblem of this moment in which night waits patiently, fires crouch unlit, laughter twitches, in which I am…you are…

"I knew Roland Rias back in the day," Raynard says, stiff-arming the cold pillar. "Talk about real. The man could see things. I loved that because myself, I don't have it in me. Craftsman me. I befriended him, if that's the appropriate term, and we've remained friends ever since."

Henry swallows an awful guffaw. "He didn't tell me."

"Unprofessional. With you coming to interview me, we thought it might slant things."

Henry tries a smile. "What's to slant in a glamour rag?"

"Ask Roland about the importance of appearances. Of the appropriate approach. Listen." Raynard swivels to Henry. "I've heard about your fuckup with the turban. I've heard other things and now I see them and you've got too much of what I never had to keep fucking up in insignificant ways like the turban, like this. You've come to profile me? Fucking profile me. Get your pen in your right hand. Divinity—fuck! What's real is what's divine! Shut your fucking face and listen: at age eight, I received my first camera and began photographing crayfish in the creek near my house. By age ten, I was doing the headshots for the elementary school yearbook. Stupid background shit. Necessary. Here's a good anecdote about how I use a Picasso-like mindset in fashion photography. It'll make a good lead and you can hang the whole piece on my Picasso vision. You fucking writing this down, you divine fuck?"

"Wine?"

She stands beside Henry, the Goddess, hefting two wide glasses of red. He looks at her, then his notes. "A hangnail," followed by Raynard's spoonfed comments on himself. The entire profile right there. Looks at her again.

"Thanks."

"Cheers."

They toast.

"Have you ever been a model?" she asks.

"Briefly," Henry says, lying. Why?

"Why briefly?"

"My dad had no respect for it."

"You could do it."

"Thanks."

"Cheers."

They toast. They look at Raynard, who sits at the table squeezing grapes between thumb and forefinger, crushing them and dropping them into a plastic cup. Into it, he pours water from a carafe. He drinks, using his teeth as a strainer. He notices Henry and the Goddess standing together in the middle of the darkened chamber, and lifts a hand. He swallows. With stained lips, he mouths the word, "Gorgeous."

"Would you walk me to the train?" says the Goddess.

"O.K."

"This city," she says, "is full of monsters."

And so Henry exits this big building not only through the gleaming brass revolving door, but with the Goddess in tow. At this hour, the streets speak of the rev up to revelry. Hardy young souls clusterlaughing in the wind-driven fog, ecstatic at the liberation that visits them day after day. Balloons on the door of a live-in art space; the hip invitees to the opening smoke outside. And everyone, absolutely everyone, turns to watch as Henry and the Goddess pass by. And everyone thinking the same thing:

Traitor.

She's got her arm linked in his, and they're walking swiftly— Henry and this Goddess who is nothing if not watched, who wants Henry because he has not laid an eye on her ever since Raynard said the word, "hangnail."

"Why do you worry about not being respected by your dad?" says the Goddess.

He picks up the pace, nearly dragging her along the wide streets. Past an empty parking lot, two dollars every twenty minutes. Beneath a freeway: nightlight piss-smell and a deafening crash-hum, crash-hum. Inside a bright, glass encased Chevy's Mexican Restaurant, everyone—again—turns with a *J'accuse* gaze to the man with the Goddess rushing down the windy street. At the entrance to the train, he cannot look at her, the disassembled features—nose, jaw, tit. She hands him a card, says call me.

That night in the Lighthouse, Henry sits alone on his deck, naked, wrapped in a blanket. The year-round Christmas lights have lost their voices. The bone-chip moon has been ground to dust and the dust scattered through the ages. A cold wind rattles his redwood branches. Inside, through the French doors, the darkened Lighthouse. Thieved of magic. Henry the Unbeliever, the Enterer of Big Buildings, once again one of All Out There In the Dark.

The phone rings.

Henry jumps, runs inside. He picks up the receiver and receives nothing. Worse than nothing. Silence. He returns to the deck. Now his skin swims. His scalp feels singed. The moon's ashes spark throughout the ages. He throws off the blanket, thinking that he'd rather freeze than sit in this blanket without Her in it. Than experience warmth without Her. Anything, without Her. The Christmas lights whimper, angels in pain, monsters in eternal torment, naked, like Henry, and alone like Henry and Out There In the Dark like Henry and, like Henry, divine.

Punk.

AUGUST 17, 1999
GLAMSHACK

IF LOVE is a hangnail then there's no difference between Her madness and the madman's and mine—between everything is divine and nothing is—because the universe is composed of madness particles and the sum of them is absurdity, and valuelessness, and nothing matters and nothing ever has and I cannot endure this—I run from this.

I'm running.

These waterborne fire trails.

Down.

In the Glamshack, I take my seat with the Plains Indian Wars book open in my lap. I flip through. I get caught up in a passage about a scout named Bloody Knife whose brains got splattered all over Major Reno's hat. "A bloody shirt or trousers may be endured," the author comments, "but a bloody hat hangs close to the face." I love the symbolism in this phrase. But time's a'wastin'. I must focus. On Crazy Horse, Custer, Sitting Bull. On the ecstatic wandering spark that was the Plains Indians before the tragedy, the tragedy that might prove She and the madman and me are not the same, that everything is not nothing, that God is.

APRIL 25, 1999
HOW WARS ESCALATE

GENERAL GEORGE ARMSTRONG CUSTER separates from his regiment and rides a hundred miles through hostile Indian territory in order to pay a surprise visit to his beloved wife, Bess, a move for which he is court-martialed. Crazy Horse, dressed only in moccasins and breechcloth, his bare body painted with hailstones and lightning bolts, ignores his medicine and takes enemy scalps, a bold gesture for which he receives his only battle wound—a bullet in the foot. Sitting Bull rides into battle trailing a long wool sash. In the thick of it, he dismounts, pins the sash to the ground with a lance (the other end is knotted around his neck), and thus commits to fighting off all comers or dying where he stands, though according to our author, the Slightly Recumbent Gentleman Cow, as S.B. was called by some whites, does have one out: a compatriot who is permitted to withdraw the stake if, at the same time, he ceremonially whips the warrior with a quirt. "Which is to say," writes our author, "the warrior was so brave that he would not retreat unless whipped like a dog."

Enter Henry. He's sitting on Her couch. She's facing him, straddling him.

He says, "I want to say, I love you."

She says, "I know what it feels like, to want to say that."

He lays his head back, sideways against the cushion. He feels Her studying him.

"My boy toy," She says.

His cheek twitches. He wonders if "boy toy" is good or bad and whether it's an odd thing to say to a man who's just said 'I love you' for the first time but he does not question whether 'I love you' is an odd thing to say on such a serrated morning.

Back up to wake up.

A babydoll rap version of "Killing Me Softly." The Indonesian bed, the penis sheaths. The letter on the wall, which by now he's read—some sort of expert mimicry filled with y'alls and we's about the nature of Halloween in New Orleans. For the "she wolf" from "yo Daddyo." The photos too he's seen by now, photos of the fiancé, a willowy youth with a fine Roman nose and teeth that inspire, in Henry, for no apparent reason, thoughts of werewolves. It's been two months since She placed that flower on Henry's table in the cafe. Except for Her voyages to New Orleans, they've spent nearly every night of these two months together and nine nights out of ten are passed at Her house and nine mornings out of ten Henry wakes to the visage of the fiancé.

The enemy.

The phone rings.

She leaps from sleep.

Henry keeps his eyes closed. It's a childish gesture, but effective. It shuts down contemplation of the fact that She chose to answer the phone at such a tender moment: sweet sleep flesh and first alarm song and sun.

"Hello?" She says into the phone.

Henry opens his eyes.

"Hey baby."

Henry rolls toward the window.

"How are you?"

Henry watches the neighbor's son and daughter squirt each

other with the hose and shriek.

"Oh, baby, I'm so sorry."

Henry tries closing his eyes again. Bad idea. He props the pillows behind his back, sits up, looks at the penis sheaths. Bad idea. He dresses, pees, climbs out a window onto a tar and gravel ledge. Her voice, on the phone, he can barely hear now. He watches the children play on the sidewalk. How he hates Her use of the word "baby." How he loves it when She uses it on him. The children's soaked clothing clings to their frail, heartbreaking bodies. He looks away, so as not to cry.

The window fills with mane.

"You can come in now."

Henry stays where he is.

"Please come in Henry?" Smiling in mock supplication.

Henry, so as not to exacerbate the situation, climbs inside. He sits on the couch beneath the window and She straddles him.

"He went to the hospital last night," She says.

"Bummer."

"He's got herpes of the eye. Inside the lid."

"Huh."

"He has to carry this cream around with him for the rest of his life. When he gets an attack, if he doesn't have the cream with him he could go blind."

A shriek from the street; She doesn't flinch. Does She really expect a response from him?

"He's been through so much pain these last few months, I never knew."

Henry clasps his hands behind his head.

"He didn't tell me. He didn't want to make it harder for me while I'm in grad school so far away."

"Did he tell you that?"

"He was kind of mad."

"Why?"

"Like I haven't been very attentive."

"He knows."

Fire in Her eyes. She cocks Her jaw at Henry, as if to slit his throat with it.

"No, he doesn't."

"How could he not?"

"How could he?"

"He knows, and he pretends he doesn't. To you and to himself. Anybody with half a fucking brain would know."

She turns Her life-giving face away. Immediately, his anger turns to the burn of Her absence. He grasps Her jaw and angles it back toward him.

"I'm sorry," he says.

"You could be more compassionate."

"It would be unnatural."

"You're so rigid. Nothing's unnatural."

"I'll tell you what's unnatural. Not kissing you right now."

And he does. And his mouth goes all saucy. And then comes the 'I love you' business. And though it would be nice if She said, 'I love you' back, for Henry that's not crucial. Crucial is the smoochsauce, the scalp swim, the chest burn, the absolute inability, any longer, to choke back the words. Crucial is the fact that even under the most adverse of circumstances—and these are mild compared to what's careening down the pike—Her jaw pore tit and only Her jaw pore tit does the poor boy in. This time and every time. Which is why he's willing to upend the universe. To prove Raynard wrong. To prove love is real. To rightend the universe.

The treaty ceding the Black Hills to the Indians in perpetuity is rendered worthless by the discovery of gold; prospectors swarm in. Families soon follow. Custer's Seventh Cavalry rides through on a surveying expedition. The Indians' response is simple. "The women were ravished," a man by the name of Bemis writes in the *Faribault Republican*, "then filled with arrows and bullets, their brains beaten out." The whites' response is efficient. "It is absurd," remarks a general by the name of Little Phil, "to talk of keeping faith with Indians." Henry's response is…

Dogged?

Long walk on a long pier, into the windy belly of the *grand mystere*. They share a beer with an old man fishing, ask him what he's fishing for, ask him what he's fishing with. Watch tankers pass through the Golden Gate and sigh into the Pacific. Bound for gems and spice. Across the bay, the city raises its skyscrapers like Mongol sabers. Late sun on the white-roofed neighborhoods renders them Greek or even East African, ancient city of seafarers and traders. A green island in the blue water, dolloped, like a fairy tale feature. That heeling sailboats do not capsize is nothing short of breathtaking.

It's cold. He's wearing his big brown leather coat. Without taking it off, he wraps Her in it, and they talk about what they see and kiss. Little, closed mouth kisses that act as periods, commas, dashes, then big open-mouthed kisses that are the words themselves. He mentions Mexico. She watches a sailboat that has drifted dangerously close to the pier. He talks of going way down, to a village he heard about from a friend, scuba diving and sleeping on the beach. Next week, or the one after that. You don't need a dive certificate in Mexico. He expects them to kiss now but She's watching the sailboat so he does too.

It is coming about. If the turn is too wide, the hull will hit the pier. A father in yellow foul weather gear mans the tiller and cleats the sheets, and his pre-pubescent son stands on the bow doing absolutely nothing but yelling, "We're gonna hit. We're gonna hit."

She says She's going back to New Orleans in two weeks. For the summer.

"It will take a month or so to get you out of my heart," She says. "But once you're out, you'll never get back in."

"We're gonna hit!" yells the little shit in the bow.

"You could do something about this," She says.

"What?"

"Walk away. Maybe I'll come to you."

"I can't. I don't want to walk away.

"This situation belittles you."

"I know what I'm doing."

"After you take me home tonight, I'm not going to think about you."

"I want you."

"I don't understand you at all."

"What about now? Here?"

"We've had a lot of enchanted moments. That's all they are."

"I don't—."

"We're gonna hit!"

That's all they are. He thought they were everything. He thought She knew about moments, that they can be made sacred. He thought that in a war like this all you need to do is log enough enchanted moments and She's yours. He thought of these moments as flames that, once ignited never went out, and that over time could bring a city, or a sea, to light. And now She says that once the moment is over, it's gone. That it's not a flame, but a cheesy flash from a disco ball. That there'll never be room, much less a city or sea, brought to light. Which means the moments were never enchanted. Not in the way he thinks of enchantment. Or rather, not in the way he experiences it—far beyond the physical.

That's all they are.

Henry staggers, as if struck by shrapnel, and then he does what a man in a war must—he gets back into the fight. He allows himself to think only in terms of losing and winning. Or rather, only in terms of survival. Which means, only in terms of winning.

The boat doesn't hit, the shit shuts up and moments later father and son are hurtling westward, bound for gems and spice.

She calls him at the Lighthouse later that night to tell him She's thinking about him, and it makes him think he's winning and She doesn't know it.

The Secretary of the Interior dispatches couriers to inform the angry Indians they must report to the reservation by the end of the month. The Indians, under the leadership of Sitting Bull, refuse. But the Gentleman Cow doesn't waste this time with carefree wandering or wanton scalping. He knows the whites are sticklers for a schedule, and that come the end of the month the cavalry will come a'hunting. He uses this time wisely. He joins forces with Crazy Horse and another chief and all repair to the Little Bighorn. And each passing day brings more warriors into their camp. And each day they strengthen. For time is their ally. Or so they believe. And so Henry believes. Time, Henry believes, would say he's winning.

Who could blame him for believing this? The amount of time he and She spend together these days would choke a horse. Urgent murderous gorgeous time. Time that arcs a backward circle and finishes in the same position worlds away. Like a giddy diver turning somersaults in a deep-ocean surge. A diver on the edge of narcosis. Time that arranges the best of days as a series of mornings—three mornings in a day.

The first the one the world allows. The alarm clicks onto babydoll rap, which Henry has grown to like. Usually he's already awake. Watching the sun blush Her cheeks, listening to the neighbor children squirt and shriek, waiting for Her to wake so that they may make love. Sometimes She sleeps in, and Henry has to employ surreptitious moves to hasten Her along—a fake snore, a kick, a messy climb out of the bed to pee and an equally uncouth reentry. He tries not to clutch at Her while she's asleep. He gazes upon Her like a farmer at sunset, surveying his field of bountiful alfalfa. He gazes upon Her like a fifteen-year-old at a strip club. It takes all his strength to lie still.

Eventually, She does wake and eventually they do make love and all consideration of who was awake first, who coaxed who, fades away. Always, She bounces out of bed too fast.

In sunlight, they walk to a coffee shop, and they sit outside eating their pastries and sipping, black coffee for him and green tea for Her. So often they talk of themselves, their situation. "I'm a book," he says to Her. "Not a story. Remember that." A reference to the need for time, and he thinks it's so well put. Sometimes She talks about the difficulties associated with being an exceptional person. How, from an anthropological sense, She doesn't just want to classify states of torture, for instance; She wants to tell stories that evoke the reality of the experience, arrive in an unscholarly manner at a place of originality. Henry believes he understands Her dilemma, he a misunderstood visionary himself. He tells Her She needs to believe in Herself, that no one else will until She does, that She shouldn't even try to tailor Herself to the world's desires because "the fuckers are no friends of yours."

Long looks into the eyes. The air around them, the blood within, warm sap. Now and then, when She mentions the enemy's name—and She does it often—a nugget hardens, restricting flow. At these times, he watches thin, midmorning, midweek traffic and feels slothful and afraid. At these times, She watches him watching traffic and sees he's slothful and afraid and either leans back in Her chair with just a nudge of smile on Her lips (the better to revel) or She leans forward, touches the bone of Henry's wrist with two of Her no-nonsense fingertips, a subtle gesture of profound consequence.

The walk back is fraught with tension: will they capitulate to world time or settle back into their own, moving, as a child moves, like a rocket through deep space, trusting that Houston equipped them with a neverending train of thrusters? The neighborhood is one of many single-family homes with yards, decidedly middle class and racially integrated and proud. Hence the flora. House fronts seeping viney growth. The sidewalk graced with vivid, disassembled features—a petal marking resembling a pink and green human eye, a leaf like an elegant arm, a man's muscular back. Which She'll bend to. When She does this, Henry waits anxiously for Her to complete the Solitary Moment and move to the next—the Moment of Including Henry in the Act. Sometimes She moves to the next moment, sometimes She doesn't.

By the time they arrive back at Her house, the second morning has begun. They make love again. And again. It's incomparable, this lovemaking. It's pornographic and sentimental. He has learned, by now, to let it build, not to compensate for lulls with emphatic behavior. He has learned also to allow Her to worship him, a thing that still makes him queasy but not nearly so much now. In fact, he's beginning to enjoy it, being the object. In these moments, She tells him how beautiful he is and it strikes him like a tickling that feels good. Always, She has Her time to be worshipped. He is the mover up to a point, then gradually title transfers to Her and She fucks him with great egg-shaped thrusts from below. Never a rhythm like this. Never before. Never, even, in fantasy, has he dreamed of the power of this event. This worship of flesh.

Afterward, they lie together. Thrusted from the world's orbit, these two, and enjoined with a brutish force. When it's time to rise from morning two, they are pressed together. Another thruster engages.

Nigh on impossible to confront worldly acts in such a state, so they go for walks, or he drives Her around on silly practical errands. Or they go clothes shopping. Shopping is a joy in the aftermath of morning two. In an Italian boutique where the trying-on process is smoothed with gratis white wine, he buys two expensive and outrageous suits She likes, and he loves them. In a department store, She tries on bikini after bikini, beckoning Henry into the changing rooms for approval. A groundbreaker, She mixes tops and bottoms—solid top, striped bottom, red top, green bottom. A Joe at heart, he likes the red top, the one that shows optimal cleavage. He tries to be cool when handing out advice in the kinetic quarters of the changing stall, but it's clear She could puddle him in a muumuu and She knows this. For these moments, though, power is a shared gift. Or rather, the sharing of it is Her gift to him. When he walks out of the changing room, he encounters the salesgirl.

"She's worried about her figure," the salesgirl says, "with that six-pack stomach. Oh my God."

"Some of the bottoms fit better with some of the other tops," Henry says coolly.

Around five o'clock, the heroin addict neighbor returns from his construction job. Actually he returns at four, but needs an hour to prepare himself for the world and that does not include taking a shower.

Henry loves this time. The neighborhood resounds with Big Wheels, plastic tires scraping against pavement, little cries. Mothers cluster nearby. Cars nestle against curbs and nap. The aroma of outdoor grills. And the light. The later it gets the tighter the light's tiny fist clutches at Henry's heart and he wonders: what is it about dusk that does me in so? What is it about the color of yellow wine? Flowers and bushes respond like lovers to this light; they blush and swell. And so does our boy.

He sits on the stoop with the heroin addict, drinking the guy's beer. She sits on the sidewalk with the heroin addict's wife, talking in a tone inaudible to the men. The baby boy, wearing the ever-present Batman cape—stained with red juice—clambers over the white fence and topples on to the concrete beside his mother and Her. He pauses, raises a wail. The little girl rushes to him and gathers him in her arms though she cannot raise him off the ground. She coos to him as if he were one of her dolls. The mother watches in mild annoyance. She watches with envy and desire. He watches with bursting breast—this could be you you you you you.

"I get paid the first of the month," says the heroin addict. "If you got, like two hundred to tide us over I'll get it to you on the first of the month."

Henry lifts out his wallet. He's got loads of cash in there. He makes a point of carrying big bills when he's with Her: never know when a romantic road trip will demand its due. He's slacking off at work these days, keeping up with the bare minimum so as not to get fired. The Conquistador, the fiancé—the World—they inhabit some other universe. Incompatible with this one. And that's O.K. Because nothing is incompatible. Everything is possible. For Henry in this moment of unparalleled well-being. Of unassailable hope. Does he have two hundred dollars to tide them over? Does a buzzard eat meat?

He peels off the bills, hands them over covertly, so as not to embarrass the man in front of the women.

"Thanks man."

"No problem."

And it isn't. Henry, in this moment, feels he's getting the better end of the deal. The heroin addict is getting a finger in a dike. Henry is making a mystical investment in his future, a future being previewed at this moment.

He sips his beer. The heroin addict gets talkative. The mother finally decides it's time for the family to retire for dinner. Women and children join the men on the stoop, exchange the easy farewells of people who will see one another within hours—people who are part of one another. Henry and Her go upstairs. He picks Her up, carries Her to the bedroom and throws Her on the bed.

Morning three is order-in pizza, rented movie, wine.

On the morning of May 17, 1876, upon the parade ground of Fort Abraham Lincoln, in the Dakota Territory, wives and children gather to bid farewell to Custer and his Seventh Cavalry. The caravan—soldiers, artillery, and white-hooded wagons—extends for nearly two miles. A thick ground fog lifts slightly, and the entire assemblage is reflected overhead: troops, children, women, and guns and mules. Sitting Bull should see this. Sitting Bull should take note of this symbolism. Though he may lay waste to the whites today, to those right now on the ground, the enemy is so numerous, so hell-bent, they fill the sky like phantoms. The question is not: will they be back? The question is not: how soon? The question is: how strong? And the answer is: too strong. The phantoms in the sky are like soldiers-in-wait and once the Seventh is rubbed out, the phantoms will take its place. Only there'll be more soldiers this time. With each passing day: more. And the Indians weaken. Because time may be their ally in this battle, but it's their enemy in the war.

And so with Henry.

Time would say he's winning. Then again, time would say he's not.

For no matter how much time they spend together, no matter how many horses go to the ground choking on the sheer mass of their togetherness, one fact remains: time passes. Or rather, time has passed. More specifically, three weeks have passed since he first said "I love you" and now he's only got ten days left. Ten days within which to vanquish the fiancé. Ten days before She heads back to New Orleans for the summer and so She tells him, makes Her *decision*. This deadline, lurking hunched, hairy and fanged, like a werewolf, turns each of their brief and minor partings into frightful severences. An until-tomorrow kiss goodbye and a hand on the doorknob are followed by a swivel back toward Her and a hard embrace. A solo drive back from her house, across the bridge, is accompanied by a careening heartbeat, a vision of that shining metallic city by the bay as oblivious to the impending apocalypse. The entry into the Lighthouse is a ginger affair, not because of the mystery awaiting inside, but on account of its absence. Each time he walks into his apartment these days, it's like entering an afterworld. A hectic lethargy infects his limbs. A heaviness of bone but a quickening of the nerve tissue. Far too alive, he is being mummified. For at most an hour he will endure this and then (a) go down the street for a drink, (b) call a friend to meet him for a drink, (c) call Her to arrange the next meeting, preferably immediately or, if a, b and c fail, pace and crackle.

He realizes, finally, that something must be done, so he scours his sparse arsenal for a bludgeon, finds one with the word "Mexico" imprinted on its business end, and sets about bludgeoning Her.

By the crimson light of his libido, he describes for Her his cut-and-pasted vision: "Way down on the Sea of Cortez there's a tiny ancient village where they bring fish onto the beach and toss them in a big cast iron pot, all kinds of fish—bonito, octopus, shark—and the fish stew while you sit there with the locals, not talking but communicating just the same, and the stew is ready at sundown and you're given a wooden bowl and a spoon like a ladle and later we'll make love in a thatch-roofed bungalow without walls."

"Without walls," She says. "Mmm."

He nods. He's almost there. He refines the concept further. Mexico becomes Baja. "Baja," he says, over and over. Way down in

Baja. C'mon, let's go.

Baja.

But they don't. She can't (damn those "states of torture!"). Though they do go to Big Sur, and they do make love in the cabin and She is startled by how swiftly She comes, and his semen, like an emblem, does seep from Her pussy and stain the tight orange dress She wears to dinner that night in an expensive restaurant with bad food perched on a cliff's edge thousands of feet above the moonchalked ocean, where they are given the finest table on account, so he reckons, of being the finest couple in the pretentious, cheeseball joint. After dinner, they sit on the restaurant's deck and watch raccoon eyes in the tall grass below them and watch them climb onto the railing with their black, burglar's paws. Raccoons, fierce fighters, carriers of disease, converge on their lover's perch as She kisses Henry, She keeps kissing him until the sauce rises in his mouth and She says maybe he will be Her "Boo" after all, providing he learns to dress to kill, and in this moment, it seems She truly loves our boy, and in this light, the raccoons look like adorable children.

The next day on the beach they walk past families and a pack of skaterats without skateboards diving down a dune, and as She and Henry pass them, She doffs the red bikini top, and the skaterats hoot. Fifty yards later, they lay in the sand, Her breasts go sunblushed, their desire edges into the red zone and eventually so does his need to pee.

She follows him into the woods, a small canyon with a smooth dirt floor and red trees of sumo girth. The beach is still visible, a white-blue gauze, the texture of imagination. He stands near a redwood and pees. And pees. She approaches him from behind, gently takes hold of his dick and holds it and he hardens and pees and She watches the flow like the passionate student She is. He pees for so long he has to laugh. She's focused, humorless, on his dick. When he's done, he doesn't shake and neither does She; as if She'd been waiting for this moment to become possible, She squats and the veins in Her wide, powerful feet throb. She pushes his dick into Her mouth and he's going to come right away so he takes a step back, up the hill, draws Her upright by the underarms and pivots Her away from him with his hands on her hips and She knows what to do. She stiff-arms the redwood while he slides down Her yellow bottoms, disengages them from Her raised ankles, lifts them free of Her upturned feet. Released, She assumes a wide stance. The downy blond hairs on the backs of Her thighs bristle. In the imaginary distance, the skaterats hurl themselves off the hill.

Custer refuses to drag a battery of Gatling guns to his Last Stand because he wants to get quickly to the Greasy Grass, as the Indians refer to the Little Bighorn region. He wants to get there quickly so he can score his rout and be back in Philadelphia for the Centennial celebration, and more importantly, the nominating convention for President. So he ignores the warnings from his Indian scouts, one by the name of White Man Runs Him, that the valley in question contains the largest convergence of Indians ever to grace the plains. Custer attacks. He and his elite Seventh are massacred to a man. The Indians, on the other hand, have the time of their lives. A man by the name of Iron Hawk shoots an arrow through a soldier on horseback, rides alongside, and whacks him in the neck with the bow. The soldier falls off his horse, Iron Hawk dismounts and proceeds to beat the unfortunate to death. "I kept on beating him awhile after he was dead," Connell quotes Iron Hawk as saying, "and every time I hit him I said 'Hownh!' I was mad, because I was thinking of the women and little children…"

Imagine the fury of the man, and of the squaws too, who walked amongst the dead mutilating corpses and near-corpses, hacking off penises and hauling out bowels. Imagine the sweetness of their vengeance upon this horde of voracious bugs. Imagine the abandon of the scalp dance that evening, the joy in feeling that maybe, just maybe, this victory means the grasses will remain jeweled, the buffalo will continue to drift like seas and the Indians will never cease their magical wandering.

Now imagine Henry. Time may be running out, as with the

Sioux, but with the pier, the three-morning days, the raccoons and the woods, he thinks—and increasingly, it seems, She thinks it too—he's truly winning.

No more than four days before D-Day, She beckons him into the shed beside Her house where Her Indonesian teak dresser is stored as well as a love seat. It's a hot sunny day, and the shed, which he has never entered, never seen opened, has the air of an Egyptian vault. Through the ten-foot high doorway, he walks with head bowed.

She bids him to sit, and with the air of ritual She conjures so well, She draws a heavy black photo album from a drawer. She nestles beside him and begins. Mother (he thinks: cracker), sister (cow), me at ten before I smashed my face and had my nose reconstructed (stroke of fortune). Fiancé (motherfucker). Dad.

He bids Her pause, bends for a closer look. So this is the madman who made Her. Same big-rig jaw. A mane of thick black hair. Eyes that spell out nothing. Henry waits to feel hate.

"He left when I was five," She says. "I remember telling him he couldn't go, that he wasn't allowed to. I remember screaming at him and hitting him, my father, with my little fists. And then he left, went to Europe, traveled around for years, and blew the inheritance my grandfather—he was French—had given him. He blew our inheritance too. My mom made eight thousand dollars a year. I didn't have the right clothes and I stole things, and my dad came back and he just started getting worse."

"How worse?"

And She tells him, how he tried to hang himself in the family's basement. How he slept in his car in their driveway because Her mother wouldn't let him into the house. He thought people in town were talking about him. He started looking homeless. He climbed through their bedroom windows, Her and Her brothers' windows—climbed into their beds. Sang. Annie, Oklahoma. Led Zeppelin's Whole Lotta Love. And he stroked them. "Fondled, I guess, is the accepted term," She says. Hard pause. "Actually, molested." Though She didn't see it that way then and She doesn't now. "Fuck the shrinks, fuck everyone—everyone who wasn't there." They didn't hear him in the skin of their new breasts singing; his tears never wet their bellies; their tragedy, their love, no one deserves to touch them. And She gives Henry a look: *Judge this and I'll kill you.* Her look softens. She smiles. The smile that occurs not on Her face but in the air around. "I used to love fishing with him. He sang to me." She rests Her hand on Her thigh. "He's why I love plants."

Henry rests his hand on Her hand. Ancient wood creaks. A spade of darkness crosses Her face. Hands unrest. Wind shoulders one of the lateral doors shut. Dad's face fades. Henry disengages from Her entwining thighs and opens the door. Light. Once again. He stands and breathes the outside air. *Our tragedy, our love. He's why I love plants.* The purity in those statements, and their apparent truth, and sickness, make him want to protect Her forever. And yet it is so incompatible with other things that he knows: the inky madness of the father, the daughter's soft, inflectionless betrayals—these things make him want to step through the door and escape. And so caught, he sits. His thigh touches Hers but lightly and with no entwining. Stiffly they sit and look down upon the photographs. Upon the old mad bastard's huge face. Made, Henry thinks, for staring down fish.

Henry checks on the sun.

He says, "I mean why."

"Why did he go crazy?"

"Dumb question, I guess."

"Not an unusual one."

Henry picks at the damp couch fabric. "Call me usual," he says.

"Usual."

"Say it without the Y sound at the beginning."

"Oosual."

"Oozeooall. Ooze o'er all. Means to ooze over everything. Old Irish."

"Gaelic."

"I'm fluent."

"Only in the language of love."

"Only?" Said with a mock frown. Responded to with a smile. And a kiss. She kisses him. They kiss. Their bodies come together like claythings. The risk in this is that they form themselves into something else altogether. The risk and the bounty. It's what he wants. Has always wanted. To be something greater than himself. He is a noble commander at the center of a great battle, fighting for his life—for their life—amidst dry light and moldy floorboards and shadows of pharoahs held at bay by fiery dust-angels, and in this brutally exposed position, he says, "I love you."

The victorious Indian army packs up camp and leaves, and along the trail the people slowly splinter. Crazy Horse and Sitting Bull, Red Cloud and Gall, Rain in the Face, and the rest of the Last Stand chiefs all go their own way. One band goes south, another east. Some return to reservations and keep their mouths shut. Not Sitting Bull. Sitting Bull leads his people north to Canada, to the safety of Grandmother's Land. Is he waiting for the next battle? Does he know the way things must go? Good Lord let's hope not. Let's hope he's like Henry—unable to peer beyond the last victory. Let's hope, in the leavetaking of the great man's fellows, in the emptying of the war chief's lodge, in the face of a terrible exile, he's unable to envision the withering.

The night after the photographs, in the pharoanic shed, She calls him late from Her emptied house, and he goes to Her, and they sit on the floor listening to babydoll rap from a box and slumber in two unzipped sleeping bags. A day later, they make love in the morning in the Lighthouse with their heads at the foot of the fold-out bed, and She comes with a sweet, high exclamation, the sound of a child peering through a rain-railed window when the sun comes out. Afterward She sits in his big black chair wearing unmatched bra and panties, emblazoned in yellow light. The white, wax-studded table, where they sat down to magic the night before, stands in the center of the room. On it, stale baguette hunks, a cloudy vase of yellow flowers, petals hanging heavy. Standing on opposite sides of the table, they dress, tracking one another's slow, clumsy progress like exhausted enemies readying for a final showdown. A yellow petal releases its grip, falls to the waxed-white table. Now the table holds three petals. Seven. They find themselves on the same side of the table. Shuddering. Embracing. Consumed in yellow light.

The drive to the airport is bleak and nauseated.

Back at the Lighthouse, he puts yellow petals in an envelope and mails it to New Orleans. He can't sleep. Goes to a buddy's house. Stands on the outdoor patio, elbows on windowsill, head within living room. On the couch, his buddy reclines, doped up on painkillers, four teeth leaner. "Focus on the demon," his buddy slurs with slitted eyes, "not the woman." Demonlike himself. But Henry barely sees or hears. He is devising strategies. One of them goes like this: move very, very slowly. There is a moment, arms straight and stiff, head bowed, that he senses…desert pavement. Razor heat. Grasshopper shudders up a dust devil. Hiss of oncoming car.

AUGUST 18, 1999
GLAMSHACK

COLD FOG. Is white the absence of color or is black? What is color? What is absence?

I balance-beam along the lip of the pool.

Fox on the bottom.

His fur's caught in the robot. His legs are straight and rigid. I pull on the robot's hose and the fox comes loose and floats to the bottom again. I go inside and dial my landlord's number and leave a message about a fox.

Idiot. Deal with it yourself.

Outside I use the blue pool leaf skimmer to scoop the fox out of the water. He's small, wet and stiff. I've seen him before. Several times. He's watched me mornings from the middle of the meadow as I walk to the shower. He's watched me nights as I drive down the gravel to my parking spot. He's observed me in a deliberate fashion. He's waited for me to arrive at revelation whereupon he could say, that's right, you finally got it right, you're free to go now, buddy.

And now he's dead.

I'm standing on the pool's lip holding the pole, the net heavy and dripping, my arms burning, and I'm wondering how in the hell this significant creature came to drown here. The robot could only snatch him on the bottom. And foxes are smart. They can swim.

I conclude he was cornered by coyotes. Hounds from Hell. I've heard they snatch babies when they get the chance. Tonight, they'll click their yellow teeth outside my window while I sleep. Eyes like moonstruck ponds. They'll say: Boo.

But they'll be wrong. Because I'm no one's boo. Least of all Hers. What did She say about Her dad? That he molested Her? That he sang cheesy songs against Her fourteen-year-old breasts? That his tears pooled in Her not-yet-bejeweled belly button? That She loved him then and She loves him now? *Our tragedy, our love.* How could I ache to be the boo of a twisted being like that? And yet I do. Now more than ever. In spite of what She told me. Because of what She told me. Which makes no sense. No sense at all. And I can't think. Or I won't think. Not about Her. Not now when all is depthless madness. Her and him. Me and Her.

I glance around. I'm looking, I realize, for my fox.

Those pond-eyed devils, I think, are not getting to my fox.

Out back in the woods, I dig a hole. The earth is soft, leafy, good for graves. The trees collect fog, turn it to drizzle. I slash at the ground, lift the laden shovel to fling the dirt and catch myself; make a pile, make a pile. I lay the dirt in a mound on the hole's edge. I slash again, this time with the notion of a perfect rectangle in mind. I want this to be a good grave. Straight-sided and deep enough that the buzzards won't get to my fox. One side sloughs and dirt dunes on the bottom. I scrape it up, pile it, make another precision thrust downward. Sweat and drizzle, they're soaking my shirt. And so chilly and white out here. What a perfect day to dig a grave.

I want more than anything to make this right. I want to make this a ritual, a truth. I can do this myself, without Her. Acknowledge the forces for and go up against the against. In this forest, edgeless and still and deathly pale, stake my claim to heat, to rhythm. Be the thruster. *Thrust. Pile. Thrust.* I want to be the agent of the event that ignites.

With the shovel, I lower him into the grave. His legs poke above the rim. I bend them with the flat of the shovel's head. The legs bend easily. I say no words. I cover him. Whack the earth flat. I give it one last good whack. All my power. My depthless madness, my love for Her, my depraved recognition of the blood-chilling beauty of Her love for Her dad. I give it the whack of the century, from which arises a revelation: this is not the way to truth or freedom. This whack of the century, it's wrong. Or at least it was when I was ten.

JUNE 7, 1976
HENRY AND THE MADMAN

HE LIMPS. His sutured thigh throbs. The shovel knocks painfully against his bony shoulder. He doesn't pause or shift the shovel or look back. How can he? The girls are watching.

Into the woods.

Like slipping through a shroud he didn't know was there until he's through, and his hair is standing on end, scalp swimming from the unexpected brush. He senses that time is different in here. It has been advanced and paused, as if whoever tends the controls realized it had gotten ahead of the world he just left and decided to hit stop, let the treeless species catch up. He also senses that whoever tends the controls is a nervous bugger, never able to wait long enough. Time here occurs in claps.

Movement goes according to war rules, army of one, no Danny to back him up. Never, he realizes in this moment, is there a Danny to back you up.

Dinks.

Heel-toe. Flatfoot. Heel-toe. Flatfoot. No pain but a crutch would help. Snap. Halt. Sound came from somewhere back and to the right. A falling branch, it must be. He surveys without moving his head, using peripheral vision. Branches, as before, hacked to spikes. If it wasn't a branch then…He hobbles a semicircle. Surveys the scene behind. The road is a black river beyond the trees. The girls are nowhere to be found. Why are they not watching? The trees, in this light, stand like slender legs, gray with fur. Pine-needle carpeting pulses golden. A vine net stretches between two pines, hauling them down. Like a great hairy beast risen from the earth. Hauling on spikes?

Look up: branches, up high. It was indeed a falling branch.

But that smell. Sour and cooked. Like burning feathers. So He cooks grackles. So what. People eat funny things. Danny eats fried bologna with mayonnaise. Henry's mother eats cottage cheese with fruit. His sister, cream cheese and olive sandwiches. He eats trees.

I am a giant.

In the air like a haze, the color green. Smoke or impending night? Roman Candle or…Mommy.

Whirl and face the Dark Woods.

Knife out and open.

His eyes are fire.

Move out.

Gait crutched with the shovel. Leg throbbing now. He watches the divot in the ground. Like a breadcrumb trail. The chunk sound of the shovel head. The underground fort. The glow of needles and the spikes of fallen logs and the gleam of knife and step and clap.

Inside the Dark Woods, it's night. Trees swarm. No gray fur now but slender blackbird legs that rub against one another, and when side-eyed, twitch. No glowing needles now but a hard, dark, volcanic floor. No knife gleam. No sun. No Danny, no girls; neither accompaniment nor watching. No mommysmell; no one to protect. No stingray handlebars; no worldly desire.

What's left?

Spikes. Pain like a bee's stinger caught in his thigh. Fear like metal filings in the blood. The rise of blisters on the shovel hand and a bruise on its shoulder. That smell again. To his left, the darkness shivers, and he swings his gaze toward it and nothing. Wait. A pale, orange glow. Sparks or has he conjured sparks? Either way, it lays his chest cavity naked to the wind. This pungent wind, which has nothing whatsoever to do with the one outside the trees. Which scares the hell out of him and he wants to hobble back to where they love and feed him, and sometimes, back there, he feels the iron presence of the cosmos lid. He feels sealed in the vault of his lone divinity; he feels dead.

What's left is what's missing, and what's missing, he feels—even at ten, he's able to thirst for what he's been implicitly told does not exist—is here, in the Dark Woods, with an event known as fire and an escapee (just what manner of establishment he's escaped from is long forgotten) known to Henry and Henry alone as the fireman.

He thirsts more than he's afraid now. Eyes of fire. This is no older kid he's about to meet, no Roman Candle. This is no thirst for stingray handlebars. This is Him.

As evidence Henry takes the wind. It's since kicked up. It gets in his nose and makes him sneeze. It sticks to the walls of his throat like tissue paper. He thinks if it weren't so dark he could see it because he feels it hot on his feet, his legs, as if it's creeping and of dwarf height. And then he does see it, the wind, lighting up the forest floor with jack o' lantern light. Soon it's rushing up the trees and sparks conjured by something other than Henry are arcing between them.

Flames, seething from the sides of trees, crawling out of the earth and racing around like a horde of red ants on the tops of needles and sticks and logs and spikes. Burning spikes. The air around him like incandescence through a curtain. Jagged, maddancing shadows. A singe on his palm; hot hot knife. He tosses it and takes a step back and lands on the bad leg and howls and the Dark Woods howl back and a great heat meets him like a frying pan in the face and he hits back with the shovel at a flame at his feet.

The flame goes underground but only for a moment. He whacks it again and the wooden shovel handle is hot. He's backwalking, whacking at groundflame. Hotshocked face. He sees it clearly, his frightful grin. He doesn't see himself in this face. That's what scares him and fills him with fever.

He tries to find the madman where He dances but his eyes sting with smoke and tears. He screams, "I'm here." A flaming branch whines downward and explodes not a foot away. Whack. He gives it all he's got but all that does is spread the flames. Like whacking a tube of toothpaste.

Squeezed breathing. Two, three backsteps. Whack. Arm hairs curling. The backs of his hands organ-pink. Prickling knuckles. Flames like rockets ricocheting off trees. Full bore brightness now, full-throated howl and incandescence has burned the curtain completely away. He watches a hairy net of vines sizzle like a bear afire. Three, four backsteps and he's able to draw deeper breaths, breaths that satisfy. He whacks a smoldering log. He hacks at a smoking spike with the sharp edge of the shovel. Hack hack hack. He must be in there. He must be in there. If He's in there, how does He expect me to go to him? With so much fire. Hack. The spike topples but the log is now aflame. Whack. Why did He appear to me before—I did see Him I did—if only to burn me back now? A joke, foisted on me by the Dark Woods, to show me just how inescapable the world back there really is? To make inescapableness a thing that hurts. Whack. He thinks of the way the world drowses when the cosmos lid clanks into position. The way he hears the tick of panic when silent inertia reigns. Knives and feet and the desire for a direct hit that can never be fulfilled, not in that way. Whack.

I want to be an escapee.

His parents are good, loving people who think the world of him and the sisters next door do and Danny does too for why would he put up with his bossing otherwise and none of it matters because no one and no thing but Henry is divine.

Whack.

A figure to his left. Three, four of them. And to his right. Big coated and high hatted. Carrying axes. With black snouts. A flash of blue light unlike firelight. He realizes someone's just taken his picture. And that these are real firemen. And that he no longer has any idea what's real. He is all alone in not knowing. He's tearful gasping laughing as he lifts the shovel above his head. The firemen are closing in, no doubt to bear him away. Just before they do, he turns his mad face to the man with the camera and shows him the whack of the century.

Flashwhack.

They've got him.

Seven a.m. Yellow sun on the screened-in porch. Henry sits with his leg propped on a chair. He wears a pair of cowboy-coated boxers, nothing else. On the table in front of him, his mother has laid a bowl of Total with milk and strawberries, a glass of orange juice and a plate of burnt-crust toast (she can't seem to make toast without burning some portion of it, which irks Henry). He has touched none of his food. In fact, he has set the newspaper on top of the cereal bowl, the better to view the front page photo of him, Henry, delivering the whack of the century. Smoke makes visual identification tricky at best, but the caption, "Wounded Boy Storms Inferno," followed by his name, "Henry Folsom, 10," will suffice. There's a part of Henry that is incensed at the photographer. The photo has the washed-out grainy look of an old image, a picture taken centuries ago. The shovel has just commenced its fierce downstroke, and the two of them, Henry and shovel, look like the hands of a clock. Ten after six in the year 1862. The face could be anyone's face. Abraham Lincoln's. Pol Pot's. It could be Dinks'.

Henry's mother appears at his shoulder. "Eat your breakfast, fireman."

Henry does not move the newspaper. He sits gazing at it and she stands gazing at him. Eventually she leaves. Henry continues gazing. No way Dinks, he thinks. He reads his name again, then glances at the picture. Back and forth, over and over. Disappointment at the photograph's quality ebbs. A smile snags his lip. A quickening in the temples. Look some more, Henry. Revel. Your form, your name. Your name, your form. For thousands to see. "Wounded Boy Storms Inferno." Thousands to admire the whack of the century. Thousands to make you real.

AUGUST 20, 1999
GLAMSHACK

ON THE LIP of the pool, I shudder and one leg sways dangerously over the water and I think: just like that. That life-altering event happened just like that. One day Henry was a normal (sort of) ten-year-old and the next he was not real—he didn't exist—unless watched. By thousands. By women. Do things really happen just like that?

They do. Wars do. Death. Revelations. One day you're balance-beaming around the pool's lip, involuntarily ruminating on a speck of the noise that is your universe and suddenly all matter dark and light becomes not only audible but understandable and says you have nothing to say and have had nothing to say since you were ten years old and the things you have said since then you've cooked up in a laboratory where the experiment du jour and every jour is to create a living likeness of a free you. Or at least you want to be free.

And if revelations can happen just like that, so can enshroudings.

Which, I realize, is what just happened to ten-year-old Henry. As if the madman, if there ever was a madman, cast some forgetting spell over the yearning that drew Henry into the inferno. Wise and kind madman, perhaps He figured this yearning could never be assuaged, that what's missing would always be missing because it always has been missing and those who yearn for what's missing lead a life of misery.

But I refuse to believe this. I'd die if I believed this. Instead, I choose to believe the madman was there, somewhere, behind a tree or a flame, and he saw the whack of the century and decided Henry wasn't ripe for revelation. Because what's wrong with the whack of the century is that it's all about Henry. Henry's image. Henry's will. And that's not enough to see him safely through the heat. So the madman enshrouded the yearning. He plugged the unearthly hole. He used a photograph of the Whack of the Century. He balled it up and shoved it in there and for good measure gave it a few of His own whacks. And there it stayed. For decades.

And now, finally, I've got both feet back on the pool's lip, and I'm balance-beaming like a medalist, and I wonder if I've ever felt so light in my life, and if my vertiginous decision to believe will help me make sense of Her—will help free me from this love, which, contrary to my mission's aim, seems to be coiling evertighter around my chest, my heart. I halt, quivering on the concrete lip, thinking of waking in the Lighthouse a week after She flew to New Orleans for the summer to make her decision, and this lightness I celebrated just a moment ago reveals itself as none other than the unbearable lightness of being.

MAY 3, 1999
THE UNBEARABLE
LIGHTNESS OF BEING

HENRY'S NEVER seen the movie, *The Unbearable Lightness of Being*, nor has he read the book, but he's heard about the oeuvre and all the fine women in it and all the fucking, and he thinks of it in terms of fine women and fucking. Until, that is, She leaves, and he wakes to a white sky, a green tree, a blue bird (not a bluebird). As if the expanse, the plant, the bird, were not infused with their respective colors but sported wire-attached paper tags penciled with the words "white," "green," and "blue."

The hour must be quite early for the city emits not a peep. Nor a twitch. Likewise inside the Lighthouse. The detritus from their last good night remains in the middle of the living room/ bedroom/dining room/study—waxed table, dirty plates, empty wine bottle, yellow petals. Our man stares at the disassembled and tagged components of the world's machinery, within and without the Lighthouse, and he feels so light, so insubstantial, that he's a prime candidate for being drawn upward, chest first, by powerful talons. When this happens, he thinks of the title of that oeuvre he once considered sexy and he understands.

Not that understanding can mitigate the horror of this, perhaps the worst moment of his life thus far. Yet even in the worst of moments, one must get up. One must pose the proverbial question: what to wear?

But this beating heart is all that's left of him and how to dress up that?

He slides out of his sofa bed. Pees in the toilet. Brushes teeth. Showers. Coffee. His heart's in a panic, his chest burns from the tug of the talons, but he sips his coffee pretending. Pretending he's Henry Folsom, active participant in worldly matters, and not some bloody shuddering sheet pinned to a wire. Pretending his only fear is of A.Z. (In two hours Henry's got a meeting with the Conquistador and the Glamrag's New York-based owner and founder, name of A.Z., rumoured to be worth hundreds of millions, wearer of twenty-dollar dress shirts, bearer of much hair on his thick arms and resident of a rundown family estate on the Hudson River. And the Conquistador has let it be known that A.Z.'s West Coast to-do list includes drinking Mai-Tais at the Tonga Room and kicking any fuck-up ass that might be malingering in the hallowed offices of the Glamrag. Kicking them into the Pacific. Abandoning them to the riptide. For the good of the family business. Which is smarting after a series of fuck-ups by one lovesick hack, name of Henry.)

"Henry," says Henry. He's sitting on his kitchen counter. He hopes saying his name aloud will give him weight. Substance. Verve. He hopes it will make the blue bird truly blue. Through his kitchen window he can see into the landlord's apartment. The fourteen-year-old daughter passes. She meets his eye, her mouth opens, she yawns and shows him the back of her Catholic schoolgirl's green dress. As if she'd never seen him. As if he weren't there. As if he were back in the pubescent Hell of married slab-shapes, living landscape of unbeing, wonky voices and nightmare laughter and werewolves and he thinks: Quick: envision a scary human. A.Z. In the doorway. With a gun. Envision something scary but real. A.Z. A.Z. A. Z. Henry Henry.

"God help me." This said aloud in the kitchen. Perched on the edge of the wet sink. Near tears. Clad only in torn tighty-whities, now damp.

Wingtips, black jeans, white oxford shirt, and a dark wool blazer. East Coast attire. In this A.Z.-friendly getup, he shuffles along a winding cement path, through a small park, on his way to the streetcar that will take him downtown. The sky is still white only now the sky is on the ground (fog). Against the chill, he pulls the collar of his blazer close around his neck and spies a tall flower. A yellow agapanthus. Agog in the fog. Joy pencilled on a tag and wire-attached to the stem. He shivers while the nightbreeze grazes his blood.

In the streetcar, he stands by a middle door holding a pole until a bell rings and the floor under his feet descends and becomes steps. The only one not in the know, Henry moves to the other side of the car. Eyes are on him, but he's invisible. A far cry from the big man who walked into big buildings through the gleaming revolving door. His chest aches, as if it contained a cold, metal rod. He glances around the streetcar, and his vision feels unusual, as if he were squinting to look through a peephole in the doorway of a big city apartment house. In a bad neighborhood. And no one's knocking on the door, no one knows he's looking or even inside. They're just Out There, milling about the unevenly lit, graffiti-laden hallway. The old Chinese lady with vegetables in the pink, plastic bag is out there. The Latino kid with the sides of his head shaved and sporting a stiff Oxford shirt not unlike Henry's. The young white guys like Henry who are nothing like Henry—at least Henry feels this way. The babes in stockings off to offices, and it wasn't three weeks ago that they would have been glancing his way, but now, they don't even know he's inside, watching them, like a sad pervert.

The doors open at Church and Duboce, an intersection that draws from two neighborhoods, gay men and thirty-year-old skateboarders and green-haired tomboys. Then the tunnel and the downtown stops: Van Ness, Civic Center (the heart of porn and booze scuzz and yet apartment ads in the paper trumpet, "Near Cvc. Ctr.!"—why?), Powell Street (the fringe of porn and booze scuzz). Henry gets off at Powell Street. There are two more stops before the bay, but those are reserved for the stockinged paralegal babes and the white guys like Henry but so unlike Henry in that they've got good-paying jobs. Cross Market Street and down three long blocks just shy of the Greyhound station to a big dirty brick building with a dingy lobby and an intercom buzzer system rather than a doorman. Shrug off two panhandlers while begging the Conquistador to buzz you in. Answer the big C's "What'll you give me, kid?" with "Please!" Give a dollar to a third panhandler, a woman. Buzz; shove and run. Punch seven for Glamrag and place hand on chest and wince and heave. And rise through bitter yellow petals.

The doors open onto a frayed carpet, and Henry walks an L shape to a room like a newsroom but not a newsroom. Scissored bits of paper are everywhere, on long white tables, on the floor. Many young women stand over these tables cutting, pasting. Middle-aged women traipse around carrying stacks of photo layouts. The Glamrag is all about presentation and design of ad space bought by people who make films and pictures and ads and not at all about gathering, prioritizing and communicating information. "Editorial doesn't count for shit," the Conquistador once quoted A.Z. as saying.

The Glamrag also employs no men save the Conquistador and Henry. There's a sexy blond (in a slightly chubby sort of way) who wants to be a graphic designer and who seems to take pleasure in flirting with Henry on the odd days he drops by to deliver a thousand-word travesty (the Glamrag pays by the column inch so Henry pads his pieces and the Conquistador, whether deliberately or not, puts them through as is). She's there now, bent over bits of paper with scissors slicing and breasts pouting. She looks up, looks right at Henry, bends, slices and pouts, and he's left peeping through his pervert hole at this woman who is not quite real, who sports wire-attached identification tags that read, "Sexy" and "Chubby" and "Blond." He's left peeping at the rest of them, these people who take care of business, albeit at a Glamrag, and listening to the whisping of paper, the clickety-clickety of computer mice, the urgent rasp in the voices of those staring down the maw of menopause. He's left with no substance save the cold metal rod She left in his chest, and a palpable understanding of the phrase, "The Unbearable Lightness of Being."

His arms are indeed hairy, his shirts cheap. He's short and his face is big and dark, and his asymmetrical wide nose has gaping olive-colored pores and long black hairs. He sports a dark wool blazer, like Henry's, with a frayed lining.

Henry touches his inside breast pocket.

"Nice jacket," says A.Z. He's sitting in the Conquistador's chair, behind the Conquistador's desk in the Conquistador's office. The Conquistador leans against a bookshelf that contains no books, only back-issues of the Glamrag. He evaluates the familiar floor.

A.Z. says, "Brooks Brothers?"

"Um," says Henry.

The Conquistador says, "The kid's a writer, not a fashion model."

"Good-looking kid," says A.Z. "He could be a fashion model."

"He's not a homosexual," says the Conquistador.

"What the fuck does that have to do with it?"

"Uh," says the Conquistador. "A lot of fashion models, apparently, are homosexuals."

A.Z. says, "You hear anything about this, Folsom?"

"I've heard, yes. I don't really know though."

"You don't know who the fuck made the jacket you're wearing either."

"I lost the label."

"He lost the label," says A.Z.

"Hell," says the Conquistador, "I've lost hundreds of labels."

Turning to the Conquistador, A.Z. says, "You do that to a pillow it'll land your Spanish ass in jail."

A knock on the frosted glass door.

A.Z. says, "It's open," as if this were his office, and Henry realizes, in a way it is.

Henry checks the Conquistador's countenance for signs of ire; nothing. Strange. The door swings back and the sexy chubby blond stands clutching a stack of Glamrags to her insolent breasts.

"Well well," says A.Z. He leans forward over the desk.

"Your back issues," says the chubby blond. She smiles not at the Conquistador or Henry but at A.Z.

"I requested them over an hour ago," says the Conquistador, stepping toward the door. "I'm in the middle of a meeting now."

"I'm sorry," she says. "It took me a while to find them all. You asked for so many, over such a totally huge time."

"Go easy on the girl, Roland," says A.Z. He motions Henry to the chair in front of the desk. "Have a seat, Folsom."

The blond hands the Conquistador the Glamrags and leaves. Henry sits, thinking: she didn't even see me. Thinking: I'm nowhere anymore. Thinking: who's he to tell me to sit? Again he surveys the Conquistador's countenance for signs of rebellion. Again nothing. Strange. The Conquistador generally guards his fallen domain with the ferocity of a kleptomonarch. Even A.Z., the Glamrag's founder, shouldn't merit such deference. Unless, Henry thinks, the Conquistador's in trouble. Or he's trying to protect me. Since when did he care so much about me?

"Folsom."

"Yes."

"I said you should ask that young lady out. Take her to a show."

"I don't know."

"What?"

"He's had it rough recently," says the Conquistador. "He's…" The Conquistador goes no further and Henry, slumped in his curved plastic chair, looks up at him. Their eyes meet, and Henry senses, suddenly, that the Conquistador knows about the wire-attached tags, about the unbearable lightness and the bloody shuddering sheet. He knows exactly how Henry feels on this terrible morn.

A.Z. says, "He's fucking up."

The Founder leans back in the Conquistador's chair, allowing his words to gain effect and in the process aiming seven long black nose hairs straight at Henry. The words are lost on our boy, the hairs too, but the number seven starts a fandangle: seven exits to Her house, seven out-of-town trips they made, seven letters in Her name not counting the last, which is silent.

"Let me count the ways," says A.Z. "Leonora Raffles, director, among other things, of a music video starring The Artist Formerly Known as Prince." A.Z. screws a finger into his ear. "You hear anything, Folsom, about The Artist Formerly Known as Prince?"

"I've heard," says Henry. "Yes."

"You don't know though."

"I do know. I know Prince—The Artist."

Henry crosses his legs, European style.

"You so insulted this woman with your arrogance and your incompetence that your superior here, Roland Rias, a man who's got enough trouble keeping his snoot dry before two PM." Again the Founder pauses for effect. The Conquistador, standing against the bookshelf, glances up from thumbing through his back issues. His upper lip jerks up and down. A.Z. says, addressing him, "Don't think I came all the way to the Barbary Coast just to stick it to this kid here."

A.Z. stands, walks past the Conquistador, who presses his back against the bookshelf, and around the back of Henry's chair. The office suddenly seems an awfully small place, and Henry notices the mess—man-sized stacks of back Glamrags in the corners by the door, like sentinels; stacks of yellowing manuscripts held together by brass clasps (film scripts) teetering atop the bookshelf. The entire bottom shelf seeps stones—fat and pale with light etchings and curved—as if they'd been made rather than formed.

Henry had never before considered the Conquistador as a full, complex man. A man like himself. What to do with that?

A.Z. grasps the back of Henry's chair.

Softly, against the nape of Henry's neck: "Donald Raynard. He spoonfed you the story and you still fucked it up." The hot breath at Henry's nape removes itself, and Henry realizes he's been tensing his sphincter. "Again, your angel here covered for you—wrote the damn thing himself."

Henry catches a glimpse of the Conquistador against the bookshelf. His lip-curtain is on a continuous jerk cycle. His mottled hands, clasped against the back Glamrags, massage one another and above, his undereye pouches hanging like gray mailbags from another century, his eyes—Henry has never before looked at those global, golden brown child's eyes—focus fiercely on the Venetian windows. Henry has the feeling the Conquistador is on the verge of crying. He can feel A.Z. straighten to full Napoleonic stature.

"How do I know all this, Roland?"

Heavy and low comes the Conquistador's response. "How. Yes. I would like to know."

"I'll tell you how, and if I hear a single complaint from her concerning the treatment she receives from you I'll fire your sodden ass and have my lawyer sue you for harassment."

A.Z. pauses for effect and it works. Henry focuses on the floor, on the stones, on the shelves, on the brittle film scripts perched precariously atop the bookcase; the glint of brass.

The breath is back on his nape. Wet breath. Spittle on the back of Henry's neck. A.Z. is quietly cackling and then the quiet goes out of it and he simply cackles.

"It's her! It's her! The girl who brought the back issues! Don't you see? Don't you know why she flies to New York on our tab? A clerical worker? I'm putting it to her and she can't get enough! She wants to marry me! I'm fifty-eight and ugly but my cock's stuck deep in the ground! That's the problem with you pansies out here. Your little dicks twinky in the wind. Me, I'm a man with his fat cock in the ground. I've got a goddamn estate on the Hudson goddamn. In the family for a hundred and fifty years. I got business interests. You think this piece of shit is all I'm worth? Ha! I've got a wardrobe by fucking Brooks Brothers." The mouth moves closer to the nape, almost kissing it. "Don't try to fool me you fuckup kid with your labelless blazer that you think just might have been made by Brooks Brothers."

Henry ekes out a, "I never said—."

"You've never heard of Brooks Brothers."

Henry concentrates on the stones; they say nothing. He scrolls up the shelves.

"No wonder you're fucking up. You think you're an artiste and your girlfriend fucks you in the ass with a dildo. You beg her to. And when she does it you thank her and call it art. Just try asking my little clerical worker to a show and she'll turn you down like a bedsheet." The breath disappears from the nape. "And you, you Spanish bastard, you Latin lover, you sun worshipper" A.Z. cackles again. Henry hears the door opening. "I'm off to get my ashes hauled and then I'm flying back to New York, where I am also king."

And he's gone. Henry stares at the film scripts, waiting for them to topple. The Conquistador stands stiffly, backed against the bookcase. He makes a sucking sound, as if sipping a drink, then reaches above his head and pushes his hand between the stacks of scripts. Three of them tumble dustily to the floor. Henry winces. The Conquistador flashes teeth. He turns his back to Henry and gropes behind the stacks of scripts. He pauses, lifts something, pauses again, faces Henry with a hunk of dull brass pressed between his flattened palms. A dull brass helmet. A conquistador's helmet.

He holds it out. Henry can see the dents. A fleck of gray, ash perhaps, perhaps flicked by an ancient Aztec, drifts from the rim and ascends. The Conquistador tracks its rise. He says, "The bartender, the mustachioed prince, he finally let me have it. He cleaned me out but I had to have it."

Henry has no idea who the "mustachioed prince" is, but he knows better, in this bitter moment, to ask.

The Conquistador bows his head.

"Why, Henry? I would spit on Cortez if I met him in the street. I would say, 'Godless thief. Murderer. Whore.' I would say, 'Why have you done this?' The Conquistador seems to address the helmet. "I would say, 'Why must I have this?'" He thrusts it at Henry. Henry jerks back. The Conquistador draws the helmet against his breast. "'Because you are Spanish.' I believe that's what Cortez would say.

I believe he would say, 'Because I am Spanish, it wasn't enough to sail past the world's borders to a country not only inconceivable but unconceived where the people—the gorgeous, splayfooted people, the monument faces—offer me meat and metals and sons and daughters. It wasn't enough to fulfill their prophecy that the god will come borne by a mighty white wing. Because I am Spanish, I had to sleep in their beds. I had to eat with their teeth and breathe with their throats.'" The Conquistador raises the helmet. "'I had to love them like a god.'" It nudges his chin. "'I am not a god.'" It overtakes his face. "'I am Spanish.'" It lifts above his head, broad, bright and arching. Point against scalp but not…

"I'm Spanish, Henry."

Not on.

He replaces the helmet atop the bookcase. He retrieves the scripts from the floor and stacks them in a way that hides all traces of arched and dented brass, of the ash inside. He turns, and Henry is struck numb by the Conquistador's big, clear eyes. Neither dry nor wet; clear. Like a field in fall.

"A.Z," says the Conquistador. "He may be crazy, but he sees things." He pushes off the bookshelf with a shrug of his shoulders. "Let's get a drink."

AUGUST 21, 1999
GLAMSHACK

I'M ON the porch, in my underwear (black boxer briefs not tighty-whities), once again chilled by the sun's retreating rays. I should get myself a corncob pipe. And a rocking chair. And a paisley print skirt. And a fucking petticoat. Then I'd be the spittin' image of Old Ma Kettle. Why Ma Kettle? Because I'm such a pathetic excuse for a man. Why do I think this? Because of the Conquistador, of course. Now there's a man. Bloodied but unbowed. Isn't that what the poet said? Fits the C to a T. I should have listened to him more closely. I should have taken his tales to heart instead of pretending to listen on the outside and whining like a toddler on the in. If I'd paid better attention, might I have avoided some of this pain? Might I be already free?

But there I go again, whining, backpedaling. You want to be free, you big weakling Henry? Start now. With your entire paisley-print petticoat being, pay attention. Not to yourself. Not to Her. Not even to the madman. Pay attention to the Conquistador. Study him. Drink him in. Look: what is the great man doing now?

MAY 3, 1999
HENRY AND THE CONQUISTADOR

THE CONQUISTADOR is doing his customary: drink two thirds of his Johnnie Walker Red and soda, order another, pour the new into the old, suck down the third remaining through the new, flare teeth. Henry, under the great man's influence, adds a shot of Maker's Mark to this afternoon's repertoire of beer. He gulps the beer first, then sips the whiskey in opposition to the notion of a shot and a beer chaser. He prefers the lingering taste to be that of bourbon. After a while, he's ordering beer just so he'll drink the whiskey slower.

He's paying for all the drinks and running low. He tells the Conquistador he needs money if this is to go on. They're in a dark Irish joint. The sign out front says, "Open 6 a.m." It's deathly quiet and the place smells of cigarettes and rot. There's a back room with two pool tables and the front room has booths as well as a jukebox playing good music. At night, this joint becomes a hipster hangout. The booths bulge with pierced promise, and the pool tables provide an arena for provocative display. Henry knows this because he's blended with these people, in the evening, in this joint. He's watched

Silence of the Lambs here with no sound. He's shot pool with the dudes in flannel shirts and the women in tight red dresses sipping bad beer from bottles. He's…

"What time is it?" says the Conquistador.

Henry shrugs.

The Conquistador leans on the bar. "Barkeep!"

The bartender, a sixty-ish man with a thousand folds in his face, pauses in mid-stoop, then continues down the bar away from them. The Conquistador looks at Henry in surprise.

"I see three people here and they're nearly dead," says the Conquistador. "There's no clock because they don't want people getting ideas, like it's time to do something. So we're at the mercy of O'Malley here and he's a sodden fuck." The Conquistador raises up on his elbows. He shouts. "Fuck!"

The bartender does not pause.

"I'm drunk," says Henry.

"I know," says the Conquistador.

"Also I feel like putting a gun to my head."

The Conquistador evaluates his depleted glass. "Woman?"

Henry nods.

"Love?"

Again, Henry nods.

"For the love of this woman," says the Conquistador, "you would gladly dance on a field of bloody swords."

"Yes," says Henry. "I would."

The Conquistador sips, and his shiny upper lip snaplifts on beasty yellow teeth, which makes Henry think of the bunny-stained canines of foxes.

"Oaxaca," says the Conquistador. "Nineteen seventy nine. Ten years I spent getting the backing to make my film. Ten years of pitches, of hat in hand. Man named Jonathon Smart, fashion photographer—where he got his start money—now Golden Boy in Hollywood. He says 'Gorgeous. Fucking gorgeous. Roland, you must make this film.'

The bartender, stained plaid shirt, still shuffling toward the other end of the bar, pauses.

"The day before I left for Mexico, I got married. You think it's strange, leaving for Mexico, on your own, to make a film the day after you get married. But you don't know this woman I married and you don't know this film. She's got a jaw like a blade, hands of an archer. Her feet splay like the hunters of Borneo but it's not from hunting, it's from running through forests. A teenage girl, piney woods of East Texas, running all out and barefoot and totally alone and at night. Night. Imagine! The passion. Think of the visions. Better than the movies, was all she said. Better than a dance. Better than the back seat of a Chevy. You don't believe in best? I don't either. But better, better is real, better is why we're not apes. And this woman I married…"

"Better," says Henry.

"Good God," says the Conquistador.

"How?" says Henry.

"Fuck," says the Conquistador. "Fuck honeymoons. My wife said that. 'Fuck honeymoons and make your film, grand man.' God, I loved that lady. Jonathon Smart, he stayed behind. He was just the money guy anyhow. Maybe, at the time, that's all he was. Maybe it was only later, after the film ground down, after he pulled out the…"

"Money."

The Conquistador, eyes on the cracked bar, signals the bartender with his third-full glass raised above his head. "I'm in the jungle," he says, "living in a tent and every day, every sweltering, holy day I'm shooting with these Aztec folks descended from the sun and I worship them, I worship how they eat, how they walk, like leopards, how they mumble to their bloodthirsty gods, and one day, maybe three months into it, maybe five, the most beautiful human I have ever seen, a man, a runner, brings this message. 'Must contact me immediately. Problem with funding. Smart.'"

O'Malley—Sodden Fuck—is standing facing the Conquistador, waiting patiently with a freshly poured glass of Johnnie Walker Red in his mottled hand. The Conquistador lowers his glass to the bar, and O'Malley pours the full drink into the old one, then heads down the bar again, empty glass in hand.

"Takes me two days to get to a phone. Some army post there to keep the aboriginals in line. Evil to even consider keeping them in line, and impossible—try lecturing the sun on the virtue of modesty. On the error of ritual killing. But the post is there, and I bribe my way into using the phone, and Smart tells me he's pulling out the money."

"Fuck," says Henry.

"Yeah."

"What did you do?"

"Flew home. Marched to Smart's office. Brought a rough cut, figured even a blind man couldn't help opening his wallet after I showed him what I was onto, the glory I had a hold of. It's afternoon. Pretty girls in skirts in the marble lobby, they all look meaner than a priest with a knife. One of them tongues her thumb and pages through an appointment book and I'm not expected. Of course I'm not expected. I told no one I was coming. I never saw the need. I'm not in the book, she says, I'm not in any book. My name is unfamiliar, and anyhow, Mr. Smart's out of the office. Perhaps I could call for an appointment, perhaps later in the week.

"I say nothing. I leave. I've come straight from the airport and I've got all my bags with me and it's dank hot like only L.A. can muster and I haul my bags out onto the street and it takes me half an hour to land a cab and I'm soaking wet now, I'm filthy, but I'm headed home to my wife and I find solace in that. I feel joy in knowing that no matter how sweaty I am, no matter how foul or unrecognized, my splay-footed beauty will take me straight to her bed."

The Conquistador breathes. His body stiffens, his eyes fix on his full drink.

"I use my key, quietly, slowly, for I'm bent on surprise, I've got her naked quivering legs on my mind. I'm at the door of our little bungalow in Santa Monica with the vines growing all over—it's like a flowered fucking nest—I'm quietly turning my key and the door opens and I can't see her but I, I…"

"Hear her," says Henry.

The Conquistador nods.

Henry shakes his head. He downs bourbon. "How awful."

"I think, perhaps, the worst is that she doesn't see me, not at first, she's straddling him on the bed and her back's to me and she keeps on and on, as he's staring me in the face and he's in total control: there's me in the doorway, there's her, fucking him, and there's Smart, finally deciding the time is right to stop this thing, to take my wife's blade jaw in his palm and turn it until she does see me. She screams and dives onto the floor and he doesn't move, he's on his back looking up at me and I'm twice the man he is but I don't move either and he says, 'Sorry chap, we determined the concept just wasn't there,' and I realize I'm holding, in both hands—presenting like a fucking gift—my glorious, pathetic rough cut."

At their backs, a hissing commences. Above their heads, a broadaxe of sun breaks across the liquor bottles. Then the hissing quits, the axe withdraws, another condemned soul shuffles across the sticky linoleum and groans into his eternal position at the bar, and the Conquistador, fists held stiffly in front of him, whispers to his liquor.

"Went back. To Mexico. Took nine thousand dollars, every cent I had. Bought a jeep from the captain of the army post. Drove upward. Found a settlement of Aztecs, pure bloods, rebels, the sort the army wants to kill and can't. How to kill an immortal? Drank some foul liquor at a plank table bar. Sun so fucking big through the door. Inside it's dog-dark. Yellow curs on the dirt floor and I'm sitting with two Commie Aztec pistoleros. They're wearing those Uniroyal tread sandals and criss-crossed gunbelts, noses like monuments. I'm dressed like a gringo with cash and they want to kill me, I know this. I love this. I would have welcomed a fight with the gods. Bartender, very large mustache, flicks ashes into a brass helmet. Conquistador's helmet. They use 'em for fucking ashtrays and I realize they won, in the end, the Sun Folks. The Spaniards might be sitting in the palaces of Mexico City but the descendants of the sun are still perched on the peaks flicking fire into brass skulls of pink heroes, of godless thieves, and I'm so joyful about this, I am so uplifted, I want so badly to flick fire and breathe as they do—breathe fucking sun—that I will do anything, I will spend my last cent, I will do it, and as I do it, I will cackle. So I say to the mustachioed prince, 'Senor. I must have that helmet. What,' I say, 'in this gorgeous godforsaken world, do you want?'"

Baby, Henry's desperado heart says, *what do you want?*

And She comes to him like a suckerpunch. Kisses that command the mouth to open ever wider, press until it hurts. Their egg-shaped rhythm and the crackshatter, the oily life inside. The blessed puddling after the storm, and after still, as if She were supporting the corners of the world for the sole benefit of Her man, Henry, they commence a languorous walking down the King's Road, wet and steaming from a new sun, through the many landscapes of their lover's realm, which is infiltrated now by Oaxaca, the Conquistador, who, Henry imagines, is bargaining for the helmet with thousand-dollar bills on the bar. One thousand. Three. At five, he turns to look at the sun. It is big as everything. Seven. The prince turns over the hero's headgear— big, broad and arching. Gorgeous. The immortal pistoleros nod their approval, and Henry is suddenly back on the steaming yellow King's Road, arm hooked around the long, thin modelesque limb of his beloved only it's not Her arm because this woman has the salad hair, the throaty pearls, the sneaky tulip breasts of the Goddess. It's the Goddess he's whiskey-dreamed onto the King's Road, which suggests that with enough bourbon and the right tragic tale, anyone can infiltrate that sacred realm, he can love anyone, he can love a motherfucking hangnail.

"Henry." The sound of his name is wonky and nightmarish. "Henry!" The Conquistador's got him by the arm.

"What?"

"One more thing and then we must flee this hell: you fuck up one more story, piss off one more director, and I'm firing you because if I don't A.Z.'ll fire both of us. I've got a duty to survive. Feature of a man."

So there's Henry, in the Lighthouse, drunk off his ass, with the Goddess's thousand-dollar-an-hour body splayed salaciously in the humid hayloft of his mind's drafty barn and a fresh assignment from the Conquistador to profile an eighteen-year-old television actress ("She's hot," the Conquistador said, "she's new, she's young.") and a threat that if this piece goes awry, there will be no more. Ever.

There he is, with puke in his throat and whumpsuck in his head and talons in his chest. He's switched on all the lights. He's paced the parquet floor thinking: maybe I should go down to the bar; thinking: don't go down to the bar, asshole. He's watched the light in the Lighthouse get whiter and whiter, the wraparound windows go shiny and hard, like snowbanks, and the arctic dark outside come a'rushing. He's cursed the evil yellow hangnail moon. He's prayed to it, mothermoon. He's turned the knob on the porch door and turned it right back without opening anything. He's turned it again. Turned it right back. Because something says Out There stretches wide and true. And something says Out There will eat your breath.

There he is, fiddling with the knob, when the phone rings.

He rushes to it. "Hello."

"Hi."

He breathes. "Hi."

"We need to meet."

"Yes."

"It's been long enough."

"It has been."

"I need to see if what I felt back there was real."

"It is."

"You say."

"Yes."

"I've got questions. Written down. Things I need to ask you."

"O.K."

"I can only go for a weekend."

"O.K."

"Let's meet in the middle. In Albuquerque."

"O.K."

"This weekend."

"O.K."

"Henry, I…"

"I'll buy the tickets, I'll make the arrangements, don't worry about a thing."

"Thanks, baby."

He hangs up the phone, walks to the porch door, turns the knob and steps into the air and…and its furred, and inside the evening sky lolls the dawn's blue tongue, and the moon's curve is a hip-curve and the redwood needles feather spiderfine and the muskywet picnic table and the laughing cherubs and the lovingly husbanded gardens of faith and the belltower lit like a city on the hill and beyond the tower, beyond the city, the sea.

AUGUST 21, 1999
GLAMSHACK

IT'S AMAZING how a phone call from Her can rightend the universe for Henry. It's amazing, too, how tight I've become with the old boy's psyche, how fully I experience his vaults and dives. Amazing and exhausting. I'd like to take a breath. I haven't taken a breath for some time now, and if anyone looked at me, if some fool made a surprise visit to the Glamshack—if, God forbid/the good Lord willing, She showed up—my visitor would be terrified of my face. I know this because I can see it, my face, floating through the house, grimacing about these bucolic environs. This reliving and conjuring, it's making me very strange. I'd like to stop. I ought to stop. Before I get very, very strange I should stop, step back, ask what I've learned, tally the answers, and based on that score, figure out how much farther I've got to go.

Simple, right? For instance, I could ask myself what I've learned about Her, and I could answer: though She experiences the physical world with acuity and nuance, which I adore, She does not seem to find within that experience a spiritual permanence, which I need. I could answer: She seems to share with the madman a similar power—the dazzling and paralyzing notion that everything is possible—but, I suspect, the similarity is a ruse, and as soon as I learn what's at the madman's heart, I'll learn what's at Hers. Or: She wants to be worshipped, yet She seems to disdain those who do so. And: Her father is a prick who mangled Her child trust and yet She thinks the mad bastard is God's gift—how mangled is that? Finally: in plants, She stands pure.

And fine.

And I should do all of this—step back and digest—but my journey seems to have come complete with its own thruster over which I've no control and it's blazing breakneck from sea to desert and all I can do right now is marvel at the vast transformations of landscape, at all the things a man can experience in just a few hours. All the states.

MAY 8, 1999
HIGH DESERT

IN ALBUQUERQUE, in the airport, Henry stands outside Her gate watching passengers from Her flight file out. He's leaning against the wall in his Converse All-Star t-shirt, the one they bought at the beach, the one that throws his chest into relief, thinking: She's not coming. Judging from the fading dribble of passengers, She is not indeed. And then She's there, in the shoes with the brown straps and the elastic olive shirt that throws her chest into relief and a herpes sore on Her mouth shiny with ointment and they kiss, and right there, right then, he feels the talons disengage from his chest with heartstopping little plinks.

They kiss again, necking this time, by the bathrooms while a little girl whose mother has gone to pee watches, and in the red rental car before pulling out of the parking lot, they make out big time. The drive to the lodge planes through high desert, the landscape of epic road trips. He talks about his affinity for this geography and bores himself and if he's boring himself what must he be doing to…But it's all right. At the lodge, a dry mountain hideaway that cost some bucks (money never an issue when it comes to Her—he pays for everything), it's urgent and She's so wet She must have been anticipating for hours and they do it with the door open. They do it while the sun grinds to dust and the pines blue and black and the tight night skin quivers like a conga and the wind rains chill-tipped arrows down from the crags. They do it until you couldn't say whose belly was whose, so mashed they are, so shiny and sticky and loud.

"That's you."

"That's you."

God they're hungry.

"I'm sorry. The kitchen's closed."

"Bummer," says Henry. He heads back to their booth where he sits, as they have been sitting, abreast. "The kitchen's closed," he tells Her.

"Baby?" She says, kissing his ear. "Baby, could you let me out?"

Through this shitkicker bar, the sole joint open at this hour, with the booths and tables and locals-only stools and the surprisingly good country band playing by the front door—never before has Henry seen a band in a bar playing by the front door—She walks. Henry has his hand on the booth's back, still standing, watching Her. It's a watery thing, this walk; or it's like pedaling. Each step has its cycle, its tense and flex. The torso rides high and straight. The hands loose but slightly up in front. The mane doing mini-tumbles, the jaw feinting right then left, the eyes glint with smile. And the locals, they follow this cyclist, this locomotive thing. Along with Henry, they watch Her ride oh so unhurriedly to the gleaming kitchen counter where stands the young Mexican man who informed Henry that he and his woman would have to go hungry tonight.

The band ends a song before it's finished, Henry's sure of this.

"How're y'all doin'?" She says. Jaw dip. Eyes twisted to full-power smile.

"Good. Real good. How are you?" says the young man.

"Jus' fine."

"That's good."

She says nothing, but the jaw remains in its dip, the smile still on full. Poor guy, thinks Henry, he's beginning to marble.

"Are you having fun?" the man says. His eyes are immobilized, pinned. "Do you like the band? Are you visiting? I live here. Do you like it here?"

"Ah love it, he-ya."

"Good. Great."

Henry smiles. He drinks some of his beer. Do it to him, he thinks. Lord, I love this woman.

The musicians stand leaning on their instruments.

The barmaid peers around the corner.

"Have you eaten?" the cook says. "Do you guys need something to eat?"

"Well," She says, and draws this out, as if deciding, with a mane tumble. "If y'all had couple'a salads with blue cheese dressin' and a couple'a ham sandwiches with swiss cheese and iceberg lettuce and tomato and mayonnaise…"

"You go sit down," he says. "I'll bring them to you."

When She gets back to the booth, She wants to make out right away—something about what She just pulled off gets Her going. Henry's honored to be in on this conspiracy. They kiss sloppily and grope. The band strikes up a train song. A slide guitar does a train sound. Train sounds, Henry thinks, are indeed lonely sounds. The concept of loneliness, for Henry, in this moment, is thrilling.

The cook sets two heaping salads and two tall sandwiches in front of them. He disappears and comes back with a beer and sits across from them in the booth. He watches them eat.

"Mmmm," She says to him with Her mouth full and tomato on Her chin. Then She turns to Henry and plants a messy kiss on his eye.

He leaves the badge untouched.

"That's good," says the cook. He sips his beer. He watches Her eat. It seems he wants nothing more than to sit and watch. It doesn't bother Henry in the least. In fact, he likes it. Mine, he thinks, and slides his hand from Her knee to Her crotch.

"Mmmm," She says.

AUGUST 21, 1999
GLAMSHACK

I'VE GOT to stop. Stop reliving for a moment. Say, O.K., what's at the base of this love? Or rather, how base is this? Sex and food and pride in ownership—is this thing, for Henry, at its base, about fucking and eating and being watched? And for Her, is it just about—wait, forget about Her. What it is for Her is not important if only for the fact that Henry's got not one spark of influence over what it is for Her, and anyhow, this story is about Henry. Farcical Henry, according to some. Divine, according to Raynard. Attractive, according to the Goddess. A pussy, according to the Conquistador. Though for some reason I sense, in the Conquistador's unevolved insult, an acknowledgement of Henry's potential. Why do you slide like a reptile, the Conquistador seems to be saying, when you've got the gift of flight? Though God knows how the Conquistador senses this since all he's seen of Henry is drinking and sniveling. All he's seen is bliss and crisis.

But perhaps that's it: bliss and crisis. Not to hand too much to our hero who, so far, fits most comfortably into the slot labeled, "Farce." But perhaps what the Conquistador sees in Henry that is good and worthy, is his ability to feel things profoundly. His need to do so. Whether that be talons in the chest, the taste of fish, the absence of essences or the kiss of some broad, as the Conquistador would refer to Her, who Henry really likes kissing. And perhaps in the feeling is the significance. The compulsion to inhabit the whole sensation is the thing that makes what looks a lot like a farce actually a story from the Book of Revelations. As in: somewhere deep in the kiss is the mute magic we know as God. As in: those who feel the thing that's missing most are the ones most able to feel the missing thing when it's no longer missing, when they finally inhabit it, or when it inhabits them, if only for a moment, and forevermore, they are divine, and their presence in our midst sends sun salving down our bitten throats. And if this is true, then Henry doesn't need to be in Her presence in order to experience all the possible sensations because Henry's got the gift himself. Henry, himself, is divine. And… Oh. Crap.

The fool's buying Her crap.

MAY 8, 1999
HIGH DESERT (CONT'D)

HE PRESSES it to Her throat, a big bold necklace, Indian style, made of mother of pearl and red stones and blue stones. He stands back, and She appears before him like some sort of Aztec deity with that necklace and that jaw.

"Not a lot of women could wear this," he says.

Her mane dip is implied, careful as She is to hold the pose.

"You should have this," he says.

"You said that about the ring too."

"It was true about the ring too."

"Can you afford this?"

Can he afford this? He doesn't think like that. He thinks: what can I say that will intimate wealth and at the same time, come across as understated yet assured?

"If I couldn't afford it," he says, "I wouldn't do it."

He lifts the necklace away, turns to the Indian woman who is sitting on the sidewalk behind her outspread wares. The street is lined with such women sitting on the sun-scoured sidewalk of the town square selling jewelry to the tourists.

"What's this made of?" he says.

"Mother of pearl."

"Oh."

"I think," She says, caressing the back of Henry's neck, "that's from the inside of a sea shell."

"Abalone," says the woman.

"Really?" says Henry.

"He dives for abalone," She says to the woman.

"Really," she says. "Would you mind sending me some shells?"

"Absolutely," says Henry. "I'm going diving next week."

"They do it without tanks," She says, and Henry turns to Her with the necklace in his hand, and She's ready for him, for his look of shock at this rare act of talking up Her man, and She gives him perhaps Her first ever full-in-his-face smile, Her first smile on the lips themselves, and Henry, standing in this high bright square with colors shining on the jewels and adobe-toned ladies sitting crosslegged on the ground and snug couples and God's-in-his-house families strolling and bending and pinching and squinting and the low-slung whitewashed adobe buildings with their timbers and their arches and their surprise parties of painted tile and the great old oaks in the square and the shadows they cast—the loving shadows, the shadow between Her breasts, the shadows of Her pores, the sunblush, the lips, the sore, the smile on his lady, who is his, She's his, he's won.

"Without tanks," says the woman.

"Do you want to get married?" She says.

"Yes."

"I'll never get married."

"Why not?"

"Marriage is an institution created to favor the freedom of the male and not the well-being of the mother and the children. He can take the house. A man will never take my house. Women need a home for their children."

"He can't just take the house. In divorces, women always get the house."

"If they get the house, they give up some other essential."

"I know a guy who got reamed by his ex-wife."

"Good."

"God."

"I'd draw up an agreement—the woman gets the house."

Henry glances over at Her in the passenger seat, and She's reading from a list of questions and the top one on this yellow legal pad says, "Do you want to get married?" and he thinks, shit, fuck, I got it wrong, and he guns the red car across a cattleguard, and She's bounced off Her fine ass, and when She comes down, She says, "Baby, please slow down."

Fat gray clouds that dogged their rising this morning have feathered and brightened. The desert's great acreage of ochre and pine, through which they greatly plane on a fresh-laid two-lane, strains toward the warmth, lifting into being, like it did the first time ever. And in this act of creation, he sees that, though he may have given the wrong answer, the trajectory of Her question is long-term, and long-term—well, long-term's what he's in it for right? The real deal and all that?

Eternity?

He thinks: marriage? Politics. He eases up on the accelerator, stretches, rests his arm on the back of Her seat, and says, "Go on, sweetheart."

"Are you willing to live abroad for at least a year?"

"With you?"

"Me, yes. Kids too maybe."

"Of course."

"Not France or some shit like that."

"Indonesia?"

"Bangladesh."

"Baby, I'll live with you anywhere."

"Good."

Piece of cake, huh, Henry?

He sneaks a look at Her to see if She's marking his answers right from wrong. She's not. She's staring out the window at a crumbling hillside, and he banks a canyon curve with a fluid motion—it's all fluid now though he wishes She'd mark them, his answers.

"Have you ever simulated fucking in a nightclub?"

"Have I…Did you…Is that written down?"

"What's it matter?"

"You can't ask stuff that's not written down."

"Why not?"

"Because."

"Because."

"Because there are rules and that's a stupid question."

"See," She says.

"See what."

"This is what I'm afraid of."

"Shit," he says, out loud—it was going so good.

"You've got these set ways of doing things. I worry you're not broad enough."

"We challenge each other," he says. "Remember when you said that?"

"Yes."

"What's broad about simulated fucking in a nightclub?"

"A lot."

"Like."

"You're doing it with a total stranger. With people watching. In a big gothic industrial space. It takes you outside your assumptions of yourself."

"You worry I've got set assumptions of myself."

"And that you can't go beyond them, even if you want to."

"Hmm." He pulls onto the dirt by the road. It's their destination, an unexcavated ruin of an ancient Native American city. Their red car is the only car. He kills the engine.

"I worry," he says, watching his knuckles go white on the steering wheel, "that you're so worried about figuring all this out beforehand because you're too chickenshit to make the leap of faith that love and any other worthwhile act in this world demands and that this

Q&A business is just some backhand sleight of hand chickenshit attempt to turn your chickenshitness into my fucking problem."

Gripping the steering wheel in the suddenly silent car as if he were setting a speed record and reading the sign that says, "Do Not Remove Anything From Ground" and trying to tell time from the angle of the sun and best guess 11 a.m. on a partly sunny day in the high desert of New Mexico and eye-burn so bad he's got to close them and be subjected to mean red dots but they're better than looking at Her right now, facing the mess he's just made.

A gentle hand in his hair. Lips on his cheekbone.

He opens his eyes to a world he knows will come at him all wonky and werewolf-like and instead…instead it's swollen with smile.

"Henry," She says. "I love you."

Atop an ancient mesa, amidst the ruins, an elated Henry—my first I-love-you! Hot damn!—gathers arrowheads and pottery shards. She reminds him, Miss Quarter Fucking Cherokee, that not only is he performing an illegal act, he's flinging rotten lettuce at spirits. "Not if I do it with respect," he says, soberly pocketing the loot. He spots caves cut into the cliff. "Caves," he exclaims, taking off running through the sage. He bounds down thousand-year-old steps and ducks into the kitchen of some ancient warrior and evicts the old fart so that he and the lady who loves him can play house. When She finally finds him, there he's sitting crosslegged by the firepit. His face is patted down with olive dust. "Let's play house," he says to Her. She laughs and kisses his face and chest and sits across from him, crosslegged. "Let's," She says. Then he tries to get Her to do it in there but She's scared, She says, of the spirits. "C'mon baby," he says, "they'd be honored." She grins and shakes Her mane so they do it instead in a dry creekbed beneath the caves. He's on his back in the sand. Kid shouts from some Boy Scout troop or other wing down jerkily from the tabletop. Above him, green leaves embedded in blue sky-gel and purple nipples frolicking and dripping sweat in little drops onto his face; She's going gangbusters up there. She's loving it. She loves him. Look at Her face, so blushlovely. So regal. Can't you tell?

Their last night, they spend in a hundred-year-old adobe ranch house with dark timbers slung overhead and walls thick enough to house—*sans* threat to the surrounding community—a generation's worth of spent plutonium. Their room is sunk into the desert clay. Their bed is a four-poster affair draped with lit chiles, the walls rough and whitewashed and on the floor, there must be thirty rich brown rugs. Into this nuptial chamber, they pass through a heavy oak door and you know what She does? She weeps. She sits on the rugged floor (cleavage!) and lets Her mane fall willynilly and She weeps. And you know what he does? He takes his clothes off. He lays on the bed, on his back, outside the covers. He admires the way the chili-light tones his bicep. He waits for Her to cease weeping. To come to him. She keeps Her clothes on, the better to worship him. She wants him to kneel over Her mouth while She goes down—up?—on him, and he puts up token resistance, which produces the desired effect. She manhandles him into position. In the shower, She brushes Her teeth, opens Her mouth, and pale green toothpaste foams down Her chin, between Her breasts, all over Her honeybellysea.

Under the giving water, he laughs and laughs.

AUGUST 18, 1999
GLAMSHACK

THE GLAMSHACK has a shower that could hold at least ten people. One enters it by way of steps, three of them, descending. It's morning. I turn the tap and down comes the water and suddenly it's the other night.

The other night, I met a girl in a bar. The singer in the band. I was upstairs in the balcony section with a friend of mine who's older and this good-looking thin girl with dyed hair was down below doing a kind of rap with a free jazz band backing her up and she was good. She had fake fur around her neck. It wasn't like babydoll rap at all. It wasn't coy or sexy. It wasn't some dead person's voice in hers. It was hard and spitty and funny, and on top of that, the girl had a solid sense of time and you could tell the band dug her. She was rapping about things like her parents new condo in Palm Springs and the bum with bad toenails who pretended to be a traffic cop at her fender bender and what the sounds the people in the apartment next door make do to her when she's alone.

She said all this in a musical way.

Then she came upstairs. I was sitting on a wooden ledge with my legs hanging off. All kinds of people were around her. She looked at me as if we'd met, and I dropped to the floor and walked and told her I thought she was really good and I meant it, and it seemed to me she was genuinely pleased. I liked the way she looked when she smiled. Very attractive. She was very attractive to me and she was attractive but not very attractive. She's got a book with those stories in it that she raps, and she offered to send it to me. She asked for my address and my phone number.

Later, she was rushing to leave, I put my arm out to touch her shoulder to say goodbye—she didn't see me—and I touched her breast by mistake. She whirled around and said in a slightly amused manner, "Oh, somebody just grabbed my boob." Then she saw it was me and there came that very attractive-making smile.

"You just grabbed my boob."

"I did."

"We'll talk."

Driving home, I felt good. Then I got to the Glamshack and I felt bad for feeling good. No, not bad so much as scared. Because if I can feel good, if another woman's smile can make her very attractive to me, how must She feel, how easy is it, for Her, without me, right now, to feel good? I'm not talking about jealousy. I'm talking about something being everything one moment and nothing the next. Or everything being everything every moment. Nothing being nothing no moment. Every being moment/no being moment. One jaw is the same as the next. Pore, tit. An Aztec sun or a depthless world of wonky monsters. Love is the anchor unless love's a hangnail and then it's meant to come loose.

And then, amazingly, the scare went away and I felt…peace? No not peace. Relief, or respite. Why struggle for faith, I found myself thinking, when there's no earthly reason to believe? Who says I've got to subscribe to my traditional religion of everything or nothing and nada in between, of martyrdom to magic or soul shriveling evolution, of best or worst? Why, for that matter, sign up with the Conquistador's watery theology of Better? ("You don't believe in best?" he said. "I don't either. But better. Better is real. Better is why we're not apes.") Why had I never before considered belief in a valueless, godless, mad, accidental boob-grabbing, Raynardian universe an option for me? Why not consider it now, under the water?

Under the water. Under the giving water comes nightmare laughter. I laugh at the terrible ache I feel when I think of Her in the shower with the toothpaste between her breasts. At the loveliness, the holiness, that I know in that moment was real. At the first I-love-you, which, sure, arrived on the heels of my answers to Her questions written on a yellow legal pad. Or rather, on the heels of me calling Her on the carpet. Not particularly romantic, or courageous of Her, now that I think of it, that first I-love-you. Not the work of the epic adventurer I had envisioned. And yet, as a wise (and hilarious) woman once told me, a woman doesn't say "I love you" if she (or She) doesn't mean it. And if She truly meant I-love-you back in New Mexico, did She mean the kind of mangled adoration She has for her dad, or something more uplifting? Either way, I realize, if She meant what She said, then my current godless valueless Raynardian respite, my bleak island paradise, my artificially constructed D-Day harbor, is blown to smithereens.

Unless…

MAY 15, 1999
THE PURPLE BLOOM
OF NEW ORLEANS

ON THE DISTRESSED-wood floor of the fiancé's New Orleans Love Nest, at the foot of a mattress bulked high with an off-pink comforter, sits a gym bag, partially unzipped, containing three pairs of fiercely lovely underwear, a frisbee, letters with lines like, "in your gaping absence, a nightbreeze grazes my blood whenever I contemplate joy," and an envelope of yellow petals. Beside the bed, melted candles cleave to a low nightstand. Outside, on the iron balcony, white orchids thrive obscenely. (It's been wet in the Big Easy, hot thick and loud, you can hear the place expand and divide.) In the courtyard below, water gushes from the mouth of a lion. Dusk arrives, a slow flooding. On gray stone and red brick, light like yellow wine. Back inside the Love Nest, the air is wan and the light is Jack and Coke. Nothing moves—.

A rustling.

A fine ass bent over a gym bag.

She rises, leaving it fully unzipped, and spatters down the spiral staircase to the first floor where the roommate lives and the kitchen is, and She steps into the courtyard, glancing at the lion whose moldy green jaws remind one of smeared toothpaste. Then She heads to a strip of hip little secondhand boutiques and buys, without study or hesitation, a black lycra miniskirt that, when unzipped, falls to the floor, and black boots with heels the size of monster truck tires. She puts them on amidst the racks of fur-necked coats worn by young women whose purses are Veronica lunch boxes. The sales girls stare but no one tells Her to take it into a dressing room. Tell those thighs? That belly?

Y'all mus' be kiddin'.

In blue floral underwear, not all that racy, She stands holding the skirt and fooling with its zipper.

"You're supposed to zip this before you put it on?" She asks. "Or after?"

The sales girls stare.

"I think," says the large motherly proprietress with the powder blue slip standing behind the counter, "you can do it any way you want, girl." She smiles, and Our Lady comes right back at her with a room-throbbing smile of Her own. Then a demure mane toss. And She slow-snakes the zipped skirt up those hardhoney legs. And She slow-snakes the underwear down.

She holds out the bundle. "Think y'all could sell these tired old clothes a' mine?"

Grimly, the proprietress says, "Oh yes."

Meanwhile, back at the Love Nest, the fiancé ascends the spiral staircase, spies the gym bag by the bed, the frisbee poking out, and approaches.

"My frisbee," the dolt utters aloud, bending to retrieve the lost toy. In the act of removing it from the bag, he sets off…

A rustling.

A fine ass bent over an agapanthus. In a breakaway miniskirt. She rises, exhaling the genuine pleasure of the flower, and then Her face falls, as if She knew the pleasure was a final one. After this night there would never again be purity for Her, not even in plants.

She strides the streets with a bitter grace, as if She'd worn monster-truck heels every single day of Her life. She makes Her way back to the Love Nest by a circuitous route. Sticks to the backstreets, the clotheslines and the unproclaimed businesses and the windows of wire mesh. Her glance is angled down on passersby if She glances at all. From the upper deck. If She can't stand in plants, She can at least clamber onto the upper deck. Where She can't be bothered with the rabble on the lower. Let them crane their necks. Hold it high and fierce, honey. Preserve yourself. You have the power.

Arrive the lion.

Glance up at the Love Nest.

A light!

Breathe. Go.

He is sitting at the base of the bed by the gym bag, hunched over a piece of paper, legs sprawled to a slack V, yellow petals on his knees, in his hair. "Your skin is my sun," he reads, "your pores my Pleiades." He shakes his head and petals fall to the dark wood. "Whenever I contemplate…" He lifts his wet face. She stands above him, girded for battle. Thinking: I could grind you. All of you. You made me!

His shoulders twitch. He squeaks. His tears weld yellow petals to the floor.

"You've killed me," he says.

She feels a thing She hadn't planned on.

She goes out. The streets have an inky shine, the night air an urgent bloat. Fire escapes clatter and sway. Liquid seeps from a black crack in a building and the building—the buildings—they're not standing straight.

"Hey hoochie mama, c'mere suck on—."

She whirls toward the voice, invisible. "I'll kill you," She says.

She walks. Through clusters of thugs and poison-tipped whores. Past families seeping down stoops. Against a red-brick wall shines a veined throat. A man resounds against a metal-grate doorway and goes down and stays there. Hooded figures in this heat, they glare at Her with glistening eyes. A lit pink cocktail glass and a trumpet and glass breaking and a growl from something part human and part wolf. The inky street is alive with teeth. The night air blooms purple like an infected ocean. Not a glint of green in the sea. Not one more glint, She thinks, forever.

And then sound goes wonky and shapes take wing and the murderess strides unmolested in the breakaway skirt and the monster-truck boots, and by and by, the sounds fall away and light does too, and She's left with the sound of Her heels and Her breathing and the feel of something She hadn't planned on that makes Her want to die and later, after more walking, more inky streets and blooming purple infection, makes Her want to kill.

It's at that point that She decides to go back home.

Arrive the lion. The spiral staircase. Heels tolling. The light in their bedroom is still on. The fiancé still slumped at the foot of the bed, glassy-eyed. He registers Her entrance with a slow lift and drop. She strides by him to the nightstand where the candles still cleave and picks up the cordless phone. And she does not leave the room, though She could. Calculate: If it's three in the morning here, what time is it in California?

Her mind is a bat and it won't do the math. She looks up from the lit telephone receiver.

"Baby," She says, "what time is it in California?"

"What time is it…What?"

"Hmm," She says. "If it's three a.m. here…"

Henry's phone number comes to Her with an image of a terrified stallion on a winter night. Slowly, deliberately, She dials.

"Hello?" Henry says.

"Hi," She says.

"Where…where are you?"

"Did I wake you?"

"I—."

"Wanna know what I'm wearing?

"Yes."

She tells him.

"I'd like to unzip you," he says.

She smiles into the phone. "Everybody does, baby."

The fiancé raises his head, and his neck rotates frighteningly far, which renders his posture that of the newly bombed, his look that of the freshly dead, and from that place he eyes Her, and She sniffles out a giggle. He's not so much funny to Her as unnatural—or supernatural—and Her sniffle is not so much a giggle as demure nightmare laughter.

"Walking alone?" Henry asks.

"All by my lonesome."

"You shouldn't do that. It's dangerous. New Orleans is dangerous."

This is genuinely funny and She laughs accordingly.

"Baby," She says, and it's unclear to which Him She is speaking—perhaps to all Hims because to Her, one Him is the same as the rest or perhaps it's the Big Him and perhaps He even quivers at the sound of Her With the Meanness of Hell in Her Throat.

"Nothing out there to be afraid of," She says.

A pause on the other end of the line. The fiancé's bomb-twisted body quivers.

"What's going on?" Henry says from California. "Are you all right?"

"You want to fuck me?"

"Always."

"That's too bad, because you never will."

"What are you saying?"

"When I come back, I'll be in med school."

"Med school?"

"Med school. I need to feel inside."

She hears Henry inhale.

"I'll be under pressure, I might need the stability of a relationship. Maybe that could be you, your role. But you still won't get to fuck me."

"What…What about three days ago? What about our room with the chiles?"

"I can't recall what that felt like."

"I love you."

"I know and he knows."

"Who?"

"My fiancé. He's sitting here with your letters on the floor. He found your beautiful letters. He knows you love me. The sad part is he knows he loves me—he still does—too."

Henry breathes. She hears it and it drives Her mad.

"You should see how people look at me in my boots."

"Please."

Nightmare laughter.

"Look," says Henry, "it's not that bad, you can't feel it right now. It's like a bomb exploded but it could be good, it will be good, it's all out in the open now just try to hold on. Don't panic. Don't worry it's gonna be all right, you—"

But She's not listening. She's thinking. So fierce out there, She thinks, so bold and taut and puddle-making. Nothing from no one, kindness or shit. Stride and infect. No touching. No one dares touch. No one save maybe a muscly pimp and I sucked his purple cock in a doorway just because he was evil.

Did She do that while She was out there?

She might have, She can't remember. Time lies in shards, one here, one there, they glint and don't touch and that's O.K., it's not scary though it is horrible. She's horrible. I am horrible.

"I'm horrible," She says into the phone.

"Don't say that."

"I don't mind."

"Baby."

"Baby."

"I love you."

"I love you."

"Please stop."

"Please stop."

"I'm hanging up now."

She draws the receiver from Her ear, places it, green face up, on the nightstand, in amongst the cleaved candles, and to the candles and the exploded fiancé on the off-pink comforter and the purple bloom that's always been in Her and Out There but never until now gurgling throughout the Love Nest, She says, "I'm hanging up now."

AUGUST 18, 1999
GLAMSHACK

THAT PHONE CALL from New Orleans was bad. There was evil in the way She planted those letters in the gym bag for the fiancé to find, in the way She called Henry with the poor exploded fucker right there in the room. There was fury, there was spite, there was intent to harm. But there was appreciation, as well, of the tragedy at hand. There was despair at the loss of Her last glint of purity. There was anguish at the sight of Her fiancé's pain. That's what it was at heart—not evil intent but anguish. What's more, now, on the Glamshack's porch, for the first time ever, I feel a little guilty for the poor guy's pain. Because it's clear that he loved Her. And it's clear that, in Her fashion, She loved him too. She loved the home and community the willowy chump constructed for Her. She loved his simple devotion. She adored his innocence and it sickened Her as well and it was Hers, after all, it was stolen from Her by him and his kind, they made Her what She is—remember: "You made me." —and if She couldn't have it She would keep it alive in him and if it died in him, if She killed it in him, She wanted to die. And then She wanted to kill. Both of which, in a way, She did.

I wish I could say that phone call makes Her evil in my eyes but truth be told, I see Her, right now, striding into the darkly glowing purple bloom, I see Her now as beautiful and noble. There's beauty and nobility in the depth of Her feeling. In Her heart's capacity to fathom the tragic. She didn't choose to have such depth. No one can. It's in the blood. We share this, She and me, this tragic blood. I don't mean to come off conceited. I wish to God I didn't have it. And I wish I could say She's shallow and mean and nothing like me. That She lied when She said I love you. That Her salient features are chickenshitness and deceitfulness (and of course eroticness). But things are not going as planned. Instead of reliving and conjuring myself free of Her, I'm being drawn closer. Closer to the fire. Which makes this next business, the business with the Goddess, a foul one indeed.

MAY 16, 1999
HENRY AND THE GODDESS

RIDING UP the elevator to the offices of Diesel Talent, Henry conjures the effects of the girl he's about to interview for the Glamrag: hot, new, eighteen-year-old star of the hit television series *Roomies*. Name of Tally Piedmont.

In the elevator, Henry hums along to Steely Dan.

"Are you with us?" says Diesel's Latina receptionist, who looks to be all of fifteen.

He is taken aback at her directness. Can such insight really come from a fifteen-year-old?

"I'm trying to be," he says. "I really am. There's just been so much…So much. This phone call. Last night. From New Orleans."

"New Orleans, huh?"

"Yeah, from…It was…I'm trying to be…You think it's working? Look at me."

The receptionist cocks her head at our mixed-up boy. "Shit yeah."

"Thanks."

He stands there grinning like an idiot.

"So who's seeing you?"

"Tally Piedmont."

"Tally?" The receptionist looks at the yellow legal pad in Henry's hand. "Oh! You're the reporter."

"Yeah."

"I thought you were talent."

Idiot. Idiot. Idiot.

"Sorry," says Henry.

"Wow," says the fifteen-year-old. "Freaky. Take a seat. Tally's, like, always late."

Tally's, like, indeed, late, but, wow, talk about talent. Turns out today is open auditions and talent means not just actors but models too. Mostly models. Tight jeans and great asses. Henry sits in a hard chair against the wall, facing the receptionist. To one side, a glass door opens into an area where nearlyfine women stand over white countertops, studying slides. To the other side, a glass door opens onto a smaller area with only one Nearlyfine who sits across from Trulyfines and listens to them read from a piece of paper. A Nearlyfine walks out of the white countertop area. (Nearlyfine, Trulyfine—these unseemly appellations are just a silly illustration of Henry's shameful ability to assume, temporarily, his environment's mindset as his own, i.e., to think as the Diesels do, or, to think that nothing is incompatible.) Her hand is on a blond man's shoulder. He's tall, and her arm angles up. She says, "Welcome to Diesel." They pass Henry and he feels a twinge of envy. This dude's in, he's part of it, he's damn good enough, he belongs.

A woman with long dark hair and a long clingy skirt sits next to Henry. She flips open a large, hardcover notebook. Pages of music in pencil. "Pianissimo." "Allegro." Classical music. Henry can't stand classical music. Comes at him like a gas. Makes him think of hot days as a kid, the cosmos lid slid firmly into position.

The woman erases a half-note, dangles her elegant fingers above the page and pencils in the same damn thing.

What's this? She lays a page from a magazine on the music. A picture of a fine woman in an evening dress, burgundies the colors around her, Italian the origin of the words above. She lays down another page—same chick only more cleavage. Another, another… Much better than classical music.

He sneaks a glance at the real thing—yep, it's her—and gets caught.

"You've got a good look," she says.

"Thanks."

"Are you auditioning?"

"Actually, I'm a journalist."

"Really?" She pulls the pages off the music. "I compose classical music. I just do this for…"

"You've got a great look too."

"Thanks."

"I love classical music."

"Really?"

"Really."

Really.

Thing is, he feels a sudden crush of compassion for this woman who's not as sexy as the tight-jeans chicks—more stately than sexy. She's slaving to support a passion. He wants her to succeed, like the blond guy; no, instead of the blond guy. He wants her to feel the comfort and well-being of success and belonging. He wants her self-esteem to rise. He envisions the geeky fourteen-year-old with translucent red hands and a black clarinet, and it's all he can do not to hug her, to cling to her, to sob into her exquisite neck.

She goes in, comes out; rejected.

"You'll get it," she tells Henry as she's gathering her things—long wool coat, magazines, gassy passion. "You've got a good look."

"Thanks," says Henry.

He's ushered into a conference room and placed across a table from a publicist in her thirties with a Betty Page haircut and Tally Piedmont, who is an hour-and-a-half late and hot and young and dressed in a bolt of blue fabric that most closely resembles an elongated tube top.

"Tell me about *Roomies.*"

"What about it?"

"How does it make you feel?"

"How does the show make me feel?"

"When you're doing the show, you're acting, you're in character, how do you feel in those moments? Do you feel like yourself? Someone else? Your character, what does she feel?"

"Feel how?"

"Emotionally."

"She's not real."

"How do you feel, in her?"

Tally giggles. "How do I feel when I'm in her?"

"Yes, when you're—."

"Emotionally."

"Yes."

"In my character."

"Right."

"In the show."

"In the show."

"How do *you* feel?"

"Tally," says the publicist.

"What," says Tally.

The publicist looks at her lap.

"I'm only thinking if he goes first, I'll know what he means by how I feel and then I can answer the question O.K.?" Tally looks at Henry. "O.K.?"

"O.K."

The publicist exhales loudly through her nose.

"So."

"Dead."

"Wow."

"Like I've been killed. Like I'm here and I'm not."

"Fuck."

"Tally."

"What else? What else?"

"Nothing."

"C'mon."

"No."

"Yes!"

"No, that's what's so bad. That's what's so horrible."

"There is something else. You're not answering my question. How am I supposed to answer your stupid question if you don't answer my stupid question?"

"Tally!"

"What!" The girl's near tears. She stands. Softly, sadly, she says, "He's not answering my question."

The publicist leans over the table (cleavage!) to address Henry.

"Mr. Folsom, Tally's upset, perhaps we could reschedule the interview and perhaps a…different interviewer…would be a good idea."

"Fucking pussy," mutters Tally.

"Another interviewer?" says Henry.

"I'll be calling your editor," says the publicist. She escorts the actress through the door, leaving Henry alone, in his hard metal chair, thinking of…nothing. Feeling…nothing. He's a rolled-up car window, an abandoned carnival, a military cemetery. He sits unmolested with off-brown drapes at his back and glamourpuss photos on the wall. The table is some sort of high-end particle board upon which perches his yellow legal pad, also unmolested. The door to the conference room is shut. There's a pen in his hand. What else? Recessed lights in the ceiling and they're on, many would say, though not Henry. Henry would not think to use words like on, off, drive, cider, sleep, wring, me. He would not think to use words at all. Words? Say vision. To say Henry "has" a vision now is to misuse the verb "to have," for "to have" something one must "be" something and being is, being is Out There. The fifteen-year-old receptionist is, like, being. The classical music woman walking to the streetcar station with her fragile head held high is being. The tight jeans chicks' great asses are being. The exploded fiancé is…being. She is being. The fact that All This is Out There is all Henry has a handle on during those twenty minutes. It's how he knows he is not. Also this vision, which he does not have, but rather, is: walls that do not enclose.

So this goes on for, say, twenty minutes, and then this: The madman in the woods is…Is the madman in the woods… The madman…Is the madman?

The madman. It's been since the "Wounded Boy Storms Inferno" photo arrived on the front page of his hometown newspaper that Henry has consciously (in the conference room, the word "consciously" is to be taken loosely) considered the central figure in this drama. Considered the question of the madman's being or unbeing. It's a question of magnificent consequence. And it is, at this point, unanswerable. All other figures arrange themselves nicely on the side of Out There, the side of Not Of Henry. So Henry is Not and that, at least, is a place, albeit someplace else. But the madman, he refuses to stay put long enough for our boy to draw a bead. Did he dance around his fire, like Danny said they say (who the hell is Danny anyway, some trumpet-blowing prophet?), or was this figure simply a tall shadow thrown by an agitated flame and what is fire anyhow if it's not a being it's an event and maybe it will occur and maybe it won't, who knows, who says, who's behind it, who's of it, Him, you, hey, chump, what do you think you are?

"Hey."

"Dead."

"You kill me."

"Divine."

And Henry looks up from his hard chair to see a security guard standing over him. Fat thumbs resting on his belt, on equipment. "Now why'd you have to go and make that cute little girl cry," the security guard says. He smiles, and Henry experiences vision number two (three if the madman is counted as a vision): the Conquistador's teeth.

"Fuck," says Henry.

"Up you go," says the security guard, and with hands hooked under Henry's armpits, he hauls our boy to his feet, escorts him down the elevator and launches him, gently, into the revolving door.

On the sidewalk, he spots the Goddess crossing the street

toward him like vision number three (or four), and finds he's utterly unfazed, and tells himself it's fate, and says, "Hey."

"Hey."

"I've been waiting for you."

"Here?"

"You're with Diesel, right?"

"Yeah," she says, easing into a gorgeous, Raynardian smile. "That's right."

In a white loading zone located on the summit of the fanciest hill in San Francisco, Henry parks his old blue pickup. He's wearing the usual, jeans, boots, the Converse All-Star t-shirt. He switches off the engine and sits gazing, levelly, about. Cater-cornered is a regal red hotel with parapets flying flags from around the world and a marble driveway festooned with limos. When the President of the United States comes to town, this hotel is where he stays. Perhaps he likes it because if he doesn't like the service at this venerable hotel he can go across the street to an identical deal. Or perhaps he likes strolling the park nearby, nodding to the sailor-suited children and Filipino nannies, ducking into the old stone structure that's still some sort of Founding Tom Cats Club. If he's Catholic, he can attend midnight mass—no fearing for late-night safety here, the rabble just doesn't make it up the hill—at the massive cathedral located at the other end of the park. He can dine in any number of overpriced bistros. He can order in a whore. What he can't do in this, the Shangri-La of Big Buildings, is what Henry is doing right now.

He's handing over his keys to a gray-suited doorman—Henry never did learn the man's name so for want of a better appellation, he calls him Jeeves—who has descended the staircase of the pinkish big building that owns the white loading zone where sits Henry's pickup powered by a fifteen hundred dollar four-cylinder two-liter rebuilt engine. He mounts the stairs to the lobby, passing beneath a chandelier. He mounts the gated lift to the Goddess's palace, which comprises the entire third floor. He hoists the Goddess's ecstatic one-year-old son, name of Whitney, who leaps at Henry when the door is flung open by the Filipino nanny, name of Esmé, who gathers up the kid when Henry hands him to her. He commences a search for the Goddess through the living room, the playroom, the baby's room, the study, the maid's room, the dining room, the kitchen, the antechamber to the bedroom, the bedroom's walk-in closet (size of the Lighthouse), the balcony off the bedroom overlooking the park, the bedroom, the bathroom, the shower with its wraparound tile bench (size of the Lighthouse), the sunken bathtub with its twenty jets (size of…).

Ah, there she is.

"Will you join me?"

Partway through, he gets soap in his eyes and squints, and making a face, the Goddess says, "Yes," and bounces doubletime, and his back slaps the bathroom wall, and her breasts, which he'd peg for fake if he knew anything about fake breasts, don't budge.

Afterward, he asks her for a dry towel. He applies it to his eyes, recalling himself as a child in the tub with soap in his eyes. He would cry out to his mother for a towel and not only would she fetch it, she would apply it herself. He doesn't know if he misses his mother, or if it's that the Goddess mistook his pain for ecstasy or that she didn't apply the towel herself or what's making him sad. He does know he's a man, a man who walks into fancy big buildings and parks in coveted loading zones and has a model for a girlfriend, a man with a gala to attend.

She's got his tux all ready for him.

"Where did you rent this?" he says.

"I bought it," she says.

"Bought?"

"You're worth it."

"Damn."

A man who commands a price.

He doesn't understand the concept behind a cummerbund. He messes with it while she dons a tiny sexy dress.

"Ready?" she says.

"Um."

"Silly."

She does it for him. He goes to kiss her, a token of appreciation, but she doesn't want to smudge her lipstick.

Why does this make him sad?

"Ready?" she says.

With her, evenings are greased. Esmé restrains the howling Whitney. Jeeves retrieves the black Jag. Pulls it into the vacant loading zone. Hands Henry the keys. He slides behind the wheel, and she hits her favorite radio station featuring the likes of Luther Vandross. Down from Shangri-La, pausing at an intersection while a cable car disgorges tourists, the poor saps gawk at him, at her, at the black Jag. They're off to a rich-kid art school built into a steep hill. A red-suited valet takes their keys. They enter the courtyard, flagstones in the ground and a fountain in the center, wine bars around the edges, wonky student art. He secures them glasses of white wine. She points out two famous bearded filmmakers conversing with one another, reveals her dream: the silver screen.

"They're staring at you," he says.

"Do you mind?"

"Make hay."

"I won't be a minute."

Her walk around the fountain's got everything but the cocked elbow and hand on the hip. It's a sharp strut, this walk, and effective; the filmmakers' whiskers twitch to the beat. Henry watches without jealousy or pride or even that-a-girl enthusiasm for he's lost in the memory of another walk, similar in intent but world's apart in motion, in spirit. He's back in the shitkicker bar in New Mexico watching Her slowpedal past the country band and the bartender and glide to a halt at the kitchen. He's basking in the smile that marbles the Mexican cook. He's savoring the mayonnaise in Her kiss.

He's slugging down white wine.

He's slugging another.

He's walking with the Goddess's right arm hooked in his, down a long ramp to the dining room *né* sculpture studio whereupon the hairier filmmaker takes leave of the Goddess's left arm and weaves toward his appointed table and they to theirs.

"I've got an interview tomorrow," she says.

"Way to go."

"Are you mad?"

"How do you mean mad?"

"You are mad."

"I'm on fire."

"Mmm. Hot boy."

"Hot," says Henry. "Boy."

"Oh. Hey." She stands and waves to a man with prematurely white hair, a flowered vest and bifocals. "Gunther," she calls, but he's already making his way to their table. He and the Goddess kiss cheeks and Henry notices they've both got a chalky film on their faces—now imprinted with lips—and that the air in this elegant hall is swimming with the pale, dry detritus of clay. Everything, including tuxedo jackets, including Henry's wine glass, is coated in the stuff.

"Gunther, this is Henry. Henry, this is Gunther. Gunther runs Diesel."

Henry and Gunther shake hands.

"Have you ever worked with us?" says Gunther.

"I don't think so," says Henry.

"I could swear I've seen you at the offices."

"Meeting her, perhaps."

"Ahh."

"What do you think?" says the Goddess.

"I think," says Gunther, "he's got a good look. I think he should come in."

"I'll take some Polaroids," says the Goddess.

"Have him bring them with him."

"He'll bring them with him."

"Tomorrow?"

"Say?"

"Two?"

"Two."

"Ciao."

"Ciao."

Gunther leaves. Salads arrive, more red than green. The Goddess lifts her white. "To a very productive evening," she says.

"You didn't tell me you were going to do that."

She glances at Henry over the chalky rim of her glass, smiles on the lips.

"Hot boy need job. Need start holding up his end."

"Of?"

She giggles. "Bargain?"

Henry looks at her grinning lips. At the embalmed diners seated around him. At his red salad. At the absence, in this world, of green. His absence now. He swallows. Nods. Lifts his white. Levels his gaze at the Goddess.

"Cheers."

Henry squatting beneath the mantle in the Goddess's white-carpeted bedroom, shirtless, shoeless, in tight jeans and three-day stubble, forearms resting on knees, head cocked, a coy near-smile.

Click.

Henry sitting in a Queen Anne chair in the Goddess's living room wearing a jeans shirt with mother-of-pearl snaps (why does mother-of-pearl make him sad?) and the tuxedo jacket, head cocked, a near-smile that's intended to express coyness but which actually appears as grotesque, post-explosion hilarity.

Click.

Henry outside at the sailor-suit-and-nanny park, shirtless, wearing jeans and boots, standing in front of the maintenance garage beneath a sign that says "Loading Dock." Something about the scene makes him think of James Dean. Or rather, makes him picture himself as James Dean (though they look nothing alike), and as he broods at the camera, and the Goddess, smokey-eyed, lowers the apparatus to her lovely sneaky breast and says, "Goddamn I want to fuck you," which delights Henry (and makes him want to fuck her) and then annoys him because not only has she broken his focus, she's scared off James Dean.

Click.

Henry in nothing but gym shorts standing on a fire escape, stiff-arming the thin iron railing like a gymnast on parallel bars.

"Ooh," says Esmé when she gets to the one with the tuxedo jacket. "Rudy Valentino."

"Gunther wanted tough shots, body shots, and dressed-up shots," says the Goddess. "Do you think I got them all?"

Esmé nods and pulls the loading dock photo from the bottom of the deck. "Ooh," she says.

Whitney wants to see but he's got Juicey Juice all over his hands and face, and he's not allowed, so he howls.

"Take the Jag," says the Goddess.

The security guard's still got that warm, tickled smile, but he calls up to make sure Henry's expected.

Diesel's fifteen-year-old receptionist looks, well, surprised.

"Hey," she says.

"Henry Folsom for Gunther at two."

"Oh, O.K., just a minute."

Gunther's office resides behind the room where Nearlyfines stand over white countertops eyeballing slides through magnifiers. Henry passes unobserved. He sits across the desk from Gunther, who flips through the Polaroids. On the wall behind Gunther are photos of dudes. Gunther pauses at the Rudy Valentino shot, holds it up to a photo on the wall—a dude who looks a bit like Henry but beefier, stronger.

Gunther calls over a passing Nearlyfine and hands her the Valentino.

"Do you think this is too close to Bruno?" Gunther says.

"Pretty damn," says the Nearlyfine.

"That's what I thought," says Gunther.

The Nearlyfine studies the Valentino in her hand. Gunther studies the Bruno on the wall. No one looks at Henry. He accepts this as natural. When in Diese…

He crosses his legs, European style.

"You know what though?" says the Nearlyfine.

"What?" says Gunther.

"He could go fashion and commercial."

"You think?"

"Maybe, yes."

"Bruno's a superstar now."

"Bruno's strictly fashion."

"That's right."

"Someone who could go fashion and commercial," says the Nearlyfine.

Henry leans back in his hard metal chair.

"Take him over to Ronda, will you Tiff?" says Gunther.

"Follow me," says Tiff, and Henry follows her through the white-countertopped room and the reception area, past the fifteen-year-old who gives Henry a nervous smile, and they go into a small white room with nothing on the walls but a chalkboard schedule with days of the week and names like Tia, Rand, Bud and Jonna. In the room sits a roller chair, and in the roller chair sits a Nearlyfine, name no doubt of Ronda.

Tiff hands Ronda the Polaroids. "It's possible he could go fashion and commercial."

Ronda flips through the pictures. "Possible."

"Come back to me when you're done," Tiff tells Henry, and exits smartly though the glass door.

"Hi," says Ronda.

"Hi."

"Take a seat."

Henry pulls up a hard metal chair a man's length from Ronda. She rolls the distance between them shut. With her face six inches from his, she studies the photos. Then she snatches a piece of paper from atop a filing cabinet and hands it to Henry.

"Just read naturally," she says, wheeling back a foot.

"Hey you: have you ever smiled at a beautiful woman with a

piece of broccoli stuck between your teeth?" reads Henry. "Beautiful woman. You—broccoli." Henry stops reading; there's a fire in his chest.

"Naturally," says Ronda.

"Broccoli."

"Start from the beginning."

"I used to call broccoli trees."

"Lovely."

"I was ten."

"Really."

"From the beginning."

"Please."

"Hey you: have you ever smiled at a beautiful woman with a piece of broccoli stuck between your teeth? Beautiful woman. You—broccoli. Got you terrified? Relax. Now you've got the WaterDrill. It's—."

"Start over. Please? Naturally."

Henry starts over. He reads it all the way through.

"You can't do this, can you?" says Ronda.

"I guess not."

"Have you ever taken acting classes?"

"No."

"You could take acting classes."

"Will Diesel pay?"

"No."

"I can't afford acting classes."

"Well, sorry, go see Tiff."

Ronda hands Henry the photos, and he trudges back through the reception area and the white countertop room and still no one's watching and that's just as well for he's a chastened child, a Fallen Broccoli Boy, a…He hoists his gaze from the floor, levels it, composes his eyes in a near-squint, his mouth in a near-smile. He thinks: I'm a man.

This ability to override the moment is a newfound weapon, a synthetic opiate, a blast.

By the time he gets to Gunther's office, Pretty Boy's feeling just fine.

Tiff is gone but Gunther's still at his desk.

Gunther asks for the photos, flips through them. He doesn't offer Henry a seat. He studies them and Bruno with more focus than before, through bifocals, and says without looking up, "How did it go with Ronda?"

"Hard for me to say."

"Did she say anything?"

"She said to see Tiff."

"Well, fashion and commercial, that could be valuable. We'll need slides, an introductory portfolio. Tiff will set you up with a photographer."

"Who's, um…"

"Paying?"

Henry shrugs.

To Valentino, Gunther says, "You're with Diesel now."

Henry's wardrobe doesn't encompass Pretty Boy attire, so he's sent to a store known for mail orders and the Germanic jaws of its emissaries, and he buys, using Diesel's account number, a red mock-turtleneck sweater, black jeans and a charcoal gray wool blazer (unripped on the inside and sporting a label—take that A.Z.!). Then he's trotted around the streets of San Francisco by a woman whose bread-and-butter photo gigs are with the fashion industry but whose passion resides in "Urban Anthropology." The tough-guy-leaning-against-the-wall-in-the-vacant-industrial-lot shot features Henry in tight white t-shirt with a jeans shirt over top. The muscles in Henry's upper back and shoulders are highlighted; he stands in an alley wearing little blue shorts and workboots and bends as if to tie his laces. The downtown sequence, photographed in the Financial District at rush hour, offers interested parties a glimpse of this attractive young man's carefree yet sophisticated side. For these shots, he's sporting the blazer, black jeans and white t-shirt combination as well as a red mock turtleneck. Miss Urban Anthropology has him striding toward her with a swing to his arms and a mischievous (she asks for "mischievous") smile on his face. Unfortunately, this complex combination of put-ons exceeds our boy's abilities, and the stares from rushers-by shame him in a way that conjures images of Her—the lioness mane, the taut deer-hued belly, the brutish incandescence—and makes him wonder if others can hear the animal groan in his gut.

When at last they wrap up this segment, it's nearly dark. The wide streets are all but empty, and Henry has run through his "That Girl" thing fifty to a hundred times.

"What do you say we go with what we've got," says Urban Anthropology, lowering the camera from her face. As she does so, a Stocking Babe and a Dockers Dude (read: normal people), hand in hand, pass the photographer and proceed toward Henry, who is standing twenty feet down the sidewalk. He's wearing the red sweater. He's trying on, for the fiftieth or hundredth time, a mischievous smile; he's poised for another run. The Stocking Babe and Dockers Dude draw closer. They're laughing, and then they both look at Henry who's half-dressed in some Silicon Millionaire's notion of a smile and fully dressed in some Nantucket Prussian's clothes, and he thinks they heard what Urban Anthropology said, the impatience in her voice, and he thinks they think he's a got-up fool who can't even walk right, smile right, and even if he could, what the fuck's he think he's doing, a man's doing—this—and they pass on down the block and he can hear them chirping and her sparking heels skid then soft slap of wet flesh, kiss, yes kiss, no, stop, lift to light-squares coming on high in the after-hours office towers winking conversation through a hectic fog revealing nothing, up there, but filaments igniting without agency though, like monsters, they do affect things. Dusk does flutter and fade at their coming. They do call down night upon this city with their vacant burn.

"Don't worry," says Urban Anthropology. "We got it."

Pan down to street level.

She's standing not three feet from his face, festooned with photo equipment.

"I've done this before," she says.

"I haven't."

"You'll get a lot of work."

"You think?"

"You've got a good look."

"I need work."

"Don't we all."

"Things could get bad."

"They won't," says Urban Anthropology, and she hoists a camera bag higher upon the shoulder and intimates a pivot toward her car parked two blocks down this inky street, which, now, as Henry looks down it, is not inky at all; it's got hair.

"One question," says Henry.

Urban Anthropology stifles a wince.

"What does it mean to have a good look?"

"In this business?"

"In fashion."

Her face, pleasantly unattractive, relaxes. "Good looking. Defined features. Features that survive being photographed. And…"

"What?"

"Honestly?"

"Sure."

"As little as possible going on behind the eyes."

Henry fingers his mock turtleneck. "I've got that?"

"Honestly?"

Henry nods.

"You," says Urban Anthropology. She's speaking quietly, as if concerned someone else might hear. Her eyes are on the sidewalk. She raises her gaze and looks past our boy, down the hairy street. To the hairs, in a whisper: "You've got nothing."

The Goddess is so happy that Henry's with Diesel she takes him to an expensive restaurant in an historic Victorian in the woods north of the city and arranges for not one but two after-dinner surprises. They're sitting in some sort of repurposed sun porch, and the waiter arrives bearing a large silver tray laden with all things chocolate. Pies, cakes, truffles, doodads. All things this restaurant makes or has ever made that include chocolate. All things Henry could do without. (He's not a dessert man, and though he's never, as far as he can recall, made this fact directly clear to the Goddess, he's sure he's proffered intimations of this inclination, and he's saddened she's never read them.) Still, like a champ, or a publicist, or a grateful beggar, he makes a dent in every truffle and doodad on the tray.

Which brings her to the next surprise: from this day on, Henry shall reside in the palace.

She issues this decree while looking down upon Henry's brown-stained mouth. Her long torso is set very straight, and Henry's still bent over his tray of delights. He leans back and looks up at her. He smiles and reaches for her hand. They hold hands over the doodad paste, and he keeps on smiling as if this were an Enchanted Moment, beyond speech. The waiter arrives; they keep smiling. The waiter leaves without the tray. She leans over the table for a kiss and gets one. She seems happy. No, she seems happily satisfied. The patrons on the sun porch seem happy that she's happily satisfied. No one under fifty at this place because it takes at least that long to amass the sort of fortune and overburdened aesthetic required of these diners. She's one of them, bestowing upon an Other. How lovely. How exciting. How big of her.

"Think about it," she says, though by this, Henry knows, she's not saying that turning down a Goddess Decree is an option; she's saying for heaven's sake and the sake of style, poor urchin, demure.

Supposedly Henry is thinking about the Goddess's decree but for all intents and purposes, he's agreed. He hasn't been to the Lighthouse in weeks. He's stopped checking his messages, and for all he knows the phone is disconnected. He hasn't paid rent in two months, by necessity not design, and for all he knows he's been evicted. He's got his truck, uninsured and unregistered, his jeans, boots, and Converse All Star t-shirt, he's got the Pretty Boy attire from the Nantucket Prussian store, he's got the tuxedo the Goddess bought him, he's got the jeans shirt with the mother-of-pearl snaps, he's got one hundred eighty-seven dollars to his name which he lets sit in the bank because there's no need to use it, not under the current configuration: the Goddess pays for meals and delights, the Goddess's fabulously wealthy soon-to-be ex-husband (she caught him making out in the playroom with her best friend, that's all Henry knows about the man and all, it seems, he'll ever know) pays for the palace, the jag, Esmé, Jeeves, the white zone, and Diesel pays for nothing yet but they will, just wait they will. As for people, Henry has neither seen nor heard from his friends, his family, the Conquistador, or Her since he stopped stopping by the Lighthouse to check his messages and his mail, and he stopped doing these things when he started getting calls from all these folks to the tune of "Henry, where are you?" and "Henry, what's wrong?" and "Henry, you pussy" and "Baby, I'm sorry."

Or rather, he stopped doing these things after two specific calls.

One was from the Conquistador. The machine tagged it as incoming after midnight. He sounded more than a little drunk, and he sounded more than drunk; he sounded scared. Which scared Henry. And since Henry was in no condition to bear up under a scare, he decided, as a man who's got a duty to survive, to forget the Conquistador and his message. Which went something like this: "Henry, you pussy now pick up the phone…Fuck! Don't you know I've been looking everywhere? A man doesn't disappear on his partners. Doesn't squander his own power. Which is bestowed. Entrusted. So you can honor all of us because it's all of ours and we're all…we're all depending. Henry. You're an affront to God. You could be better. Better than me, when I was up there with the Aztecs, breathing, sun. You've got it in you. Carry it back and breathe it down our throats. Never could figure that out. I'm old now, Henry, brother, son. I crawl to work at a glamour rag, sun stuck in my fucking throat."

The second message was a grand protestation of love and loss and regret delivered live, as She speaks, into the answering machine at night—the circuitry tagged the time of impact as morning, two days after the Conquistador's rant—while Henry stood inside the dark and wonky Lighthouse with its enchanted moments now mutated into monsters only visible when side-eyed and even then they mutate again, and it dawned on him that this place housed the inky core of a sinister conspiracy designed to kill him, and that all he had to do was leave it, and fully remove himself to a world where reality culminates in Polaroids and he'd be safe.

Henry and the Goddess. They have sex, eat dinners, take Whitney to the park, and sometimes late at night Henry paces the palace alone.

Sex: The Goddess tells her friends that Henry's the best lover she's ever had and he accepts this as true, though if he thought about it, which he doesn't, he'd realize it is true because it's wholly geared toward her satisfaction. She likes oral sex all the way to climax followed by the dog, all the time, every time, and that's what she gets, morning and night. Only once did she shake things up and that was at the very beginning, before Henry was spending entire nights, and the Goddess's soon to be ex-mother-in-law was staying in the palace. Henry and the Goddess had been out to dinner. They came home after ten. The Goddess had some notion that even though she hated the mother-in-law's son, the women could go on, family style. The mother-in-law had some notion that she was going to convince the Goddess to take back her son. When Henry and the Goddess walked in from dinner, the latter became all too clear. The mother-in-law met them at the door and suggested to Henry that he leave and to the Goddess, she said, "I'll be waiting for you in the playroom to speak about my son." This incensed the Goddess and she said, "Lovely," and she took Henry's hand and led him into the bedroom and without closing the door stripped to a little bowling shirt, unbuttoned, took him by the shoulders and pushed him into a sitting position on the edge of the bed, yanked his pants down and straddled his lap with her fist in her teeth. It was the first and last time she ever came through intercourse, and Henry was so surprised he forgot to have fun until she was done, and then he flipped her onto her back, on the bed, and completed the transaction standing up thinking that her lifted feet looked like shiny pink paddles, thinking that the mother-in-law was still waiting in the playroom to discuss the son. (The part that came afterwards, where she ran to wrench Whitney from his sleep and paced the palace crying and clutching the dazed and terrified child and screaming to the mother-in-law who was matching her pace for mad pace, "I would die for this child, you ugly bitch!"—that part Henry doesn't think about at all.)

Dinners: When they can't decide where to go they resort to a sushi restaurant where the rice-and-plate-throwing Whitney is welcome and she tips forty percent. They went here on one of their first dates and she got tipsy on Chardonnay and told Henry her son was the only human being in the world she'd throw herself in front of a car for, and afterward, on the way to the Jag, she and Henry kissed, Whitney threw a fit, and she pulled away.

And when they really can't decide where to go, they resort to a ballroom-sized restaurant with a bar running its length and a man in the center playing Cole Porter on a grand piano and a raised section where they sit like VIPs on account of the ex-husband's fortune and the Diesel-look which gets some play in this place that is all about getting play, and Henry eats brains for the first time though he figures it could have been anything, so soaked in sauce it was, and once one of her friends who lives in Aspen and takes an "oxygenation" constitutional every morning accompanies them to the VIP section, and she's accompanied by a man twice her age, and she makes a pass at Henry and later the Goddess says, "How could she have done that? What if I'm in love with you?" The last time they enter the ballroom they don't dine because no table's available and the Goddess has a crying fit over this and makes a scene about how this never happened with her husband and why does she need to be with her husband to get a table to get respect and she vows never to return and even Henry, in his deceased state, senses a general crumbling.

The park: They're a family. Especially on Sunday mornings after sex and coffee. Henry and Esmé, the Goddess and Whitney, they amble across the street with a hidey-ho from Jeeves. Esmé installs herself on a sunny bench and the Goddess, in her thong, on a blanket on the grass. Henry hoists Whitney up to a pair of rings and holds him while he hangs and laughs. He pushes Whitney on the swing and does gymnastics on the jungle gym for the entranced kid and a lusty Goddess raised on one elbow in her sunglasses and her thong. Henry catches Whitney at the bottom of the slide and returns stolen toys to their tiny rightful owners and carries the sleeping or screaming Whitney back to the palace when the play is done and whether the kid's smashing his forehead into Henry's clavicle or resting an angelic brow upon his shoulder, Henry, in these moments, pretends they are his to keep and feels something going on behind the eyes.

Pacing: He feels it too, in a different fashion, in those increasingly frequent moments late at night after the Goddess has been serviced and rolled over to sleep—or so he wants to believe—and Henry has slunk from the bed, donned trousers, and tiptoed to the living room, to the oak liquor cabinet, where the Goddess keeps her stash of bourbon and, dispensing with the glass, he paces the curved perimeter of the palace looking down upon the hotel entryways, the husbands and wives and the high-class whores alighting, the warm, curtained hotel windows, and he listens to the doormen whistling like waterbirds for taxis at all hours. He eyes the streetlights, the hair and ink, the abandonment, sips, walks, and wonders if anyone can see him up here in the palace and if they envy him, if he's enviable, fine figure of an invisible man, stops in the unused dining room with its dusty silver service like the dome of a temple and presses himself against the apex of the window's curve. Here comes a whore not dressed like a whore but you can tell. It's three a.m. The doorman nods as she descends the steps to the marble driveway beneath the world's flags but he does not whistle for a cab and she keeps on walking strong, proud woman, noble whore (don't need no cab got a line right into God). You can hear her heels through the glass, you can see her big-boned face—lady look up, see me, tell me I'm here, smile at me in that way that says things are all right and then she does it, she looks up, smiles, just for me, big smile, big-boned face, big hands too, veined and sparked beneath the streetlight's sulfurous riot like a man's hands, a man's face, she's a man, a man's down there mouthing words over and over accompanied each time by a face thrust and a kiss, and when Henry gets it, he steps back from the window and slugs bourbon and lifts the silver dome from the service and places it over his face and breathes deep wet breaths but he can't douse the fire behind his eyes kindled/rekindled by this madman who won't stop calling him divine.

Breakfast is over. Esmé has whisked Whitney off to Gymboree. Henry and the Goddess stand over the kitchen counter eyeing the slides that have just arrived by messenger from Diesel. It's Henry's introductory portfolio, processed and complete. The Goddess is particularly interested in the red-mock-turtleneck-mischievous-grin shot.

"I didn't know you had this look," she says.

"What look?"

She holds a slide up to the light. "This—."

The phone rings. The Goddess lifts the receiver and says, "Hello." She's still holding up the slide. She lowers it. Turns to Henry. Presses the receiver to her ample breast. Stares at him.

"Me?" he mouths.

The Goddess nods. They watch one another. Never before has Henry received a phone call in the palace. In fact, never has any element of Henry Before the Goddess been introduced into Henry and the Goddess. By not asking she has decreed: never. As if she knew the outcome of asking would be the end.

The Goddess waits, phone pressed to breast. She's wearing a short, thin robe, cleavage all over the place. Morning sex is yet to come. And the introductory portfolio, it's processed and complete.

It's ready to roll. Valentino, you're ready to roll. Roll Rudy roll.

Their gaze is locked and level as Henry gently lifts the phone from the Goddess's breast.

On the phone line, a ragged nasal breath. The Conquistador's.

"How?" says Henry.

"Raynard."

Henry's gaze trails down the Goddess's thousand-dollar-an-hour body, which might as well have a sign on it that says, "Raynard's Been Here." Henry smiles and she does not smile back.

"I'm calling," the Conquistador says, "to offer you an assignment. On the magazine. Don't worry about A.Z. That gilded lunatic couldn't edit a byline without my help and he knows it."

"What assignment?"

"She's been calling," says the Conquistador.

"Who?"

"Me."

"Who?"

"The woman," says the Conquistador, "for whom you would gladly dance on a field of bloody swords."

The Goddess pulls her robe closed.

"The assignment," says the Conquistador, "requires travel to the great state of Georgia."

"Atlanta," says Henry.

"Atlanta."

The Goddess stands and crosses the kitchen to the sink. Had she overheard that word? *Atlanta*. Like Baja. In sound and feel. The Goddess opens the dishwasher and begins noisily placing dishes on shelves. It's the first time Henry has ever seen her put away a dish, and it makes him want to go to her, sidle up from behind and wrap his arms around her waist in an oddly unsexual way, nuzzle her neck, tell her everything's going to be O.K., he will accompany her into the Valley of the Shadow of Valentino because, well, he's with Diesel now.

The Goddess finishes the dishes. She disappears into the bedroom. Henry does not move.

"So," says the Conquistador. "What's it gonna be?"

PAUL COHEN

AUGUST 19, 1999
GLAMSHACK

UP THE HILL, at the Glamshack, I'm alone with the deer and the foxes and coyotes but down here in a parking lot that appears to accept only drivers of BMW's, Range Rovers, paint-splattered pickups, and the odd Hummer, outside a grocery store that plays classical music inside and out, like a leaky gas chamber, they don't know what to make of me. The blond wives and the carpenters, the olive au pairs, they eye me as I sit chewing my tuna on the open tailgate of my truck. Contractor, slacker, celebrity, thief? It used to bug me, the wary attention. Then I saw the humor in it. Now it's downright exhilarating. It makes me feel like I've got the power to be anyone I want, like I could give a hoot what anybody thinks. "Yeah lady I'm a thief, and I've been casing your Glammansion for the past three weeks so…watch out!"

Hell, I could even tell them the truth if I wanted.

Well, see, actually, I work for a glamrag, phone interviews mostly these days from my cottage up the hill my editor got for me for free from some rich person who lives in a bigger house farther up the hill, I've never seen him, her, them. See I got evicted and I lost my job but I got it back thankfully, in fact, I never lost it in the first place,

I just thought I lost it, and anyhow here I am, I'm still here, nine days into it and worse off than when I started. Way worse. Which is to say, if such a thing can be said, way more in love with Her.

How did this happen? This conjuring and reliving has thrown into relief truths (the way that olive t-shirt does Her breasts) about Her chickenshit side, Her deceitful side, Her perversity. For instance, I've just born witness to the notion that me and the fiancé, for Her, are one love. Two men, one love. The fiancé's the homefire, the wildfire's me. Which is perfect, for Her for whom nothing is incompatible. For Her for whom men are rotting parts to be sewn and jolted into Her very own shocked monster.

And yet other truths have come into view. About—there's no other word for it—Her godly side. About Her noble lust for the perfect, the godly, love. How many people profess to be in love all the while knowing they're too chickenshit to even try? How many have settled for comfort or security or propriety? How many realize, on some language-less level, that by settling they've planted a loogie right between god's white-gold eyes? Millions. Billions.

But not Her.

When the call comes down to love, She loves. From deep in her seabelly. Through brutish pores. Up to flaming mane and down to orange toenails, no matter the risk of mangling. Which helps me understand, somewhat, the love She has for Her father, that murmuring demon. Up to now, I'd seen this love as dark, self-killing, like a muck-black pond into whose excremental waters She wades and disappears. But now—now I envision it as a thundercloud underlit by a silver sun. Beneath this awful majesty She stands disfigured, unbowed, gorgeous.

I am in awe.

How did this happen?

The high school kids have arrived for lunch. Colts in strappy sandals, driving Goddess convertibles. Time to wrap my tuna, urge my blue rebuilt out of this parking lot, past the mail/venture capital/ optometry center. Right onto a flat and lovely road bordered on one side by woods and gated driveways, on the other by an equestrian

meadow though it's no meadow now, not if you measure a meadow by its grasses. I've seen meadows with grass so thick and green and bejeweled by waterbeads you'd think you were dead. These grasses are so parched that wind incinerates the blond stalks, hooves bury the ashes under earth the color and consistency of brick. Hell, slam a car door in this heat and the sky will fall.

Past the sheriff and his old hat speed trap. Past the wooden Smokey Bear sign that reads, "Fire Danger Today: Extreme." Right. Right again and up. Narrow to a forest-darkened one-and-a-half lane sidewinder. Some people beep around the corners; I simply hug the edges and gun my underpowered eyesore, bracing for a shave; bracing, anticipating, who defines the line? One point three miles, that's what I'd tell people if they ever came to see me, that's what I told Her. Nine days ago. One point three and left onto gravel. Mangle gravel. Stop and get out fast before meltdown.

Slam.

The sky does not fall but it does, in this white-spider heat, drop. And catch. And hover. Waiting. For me. To move. To think. How can She be both chickenshit and noble, disfigured and beautiful, awful and divine? Is love's true face two-faced and the consequent earthenheaven blend a bitter-sweet-musty-tangled root heretofore hidden from my Pleiades gaze, and have I already lost my struggle to get free of Her, and what did the madman mean about Henry being of the madman being of fire, and why did the Conquistador save Henry from the Goddess only to fling him back into fire—back into the war—and why do I say the Conquistador saved Henry when in fact the Spaniard just presented the sword-like notion and Henry, for the first time in his miserable existence, embraced his fate and seized that sword and with head down and banners aloft marched back into the war. The war whose ending, I recall now, depends on a cold blue marble.

I pause on the Glamshack steps. *The cold blue marble.* Might this marble, like a secret last-ditch weapon, breathe new life into my struggle? Might Henry's ending finally set me free?

JULY 23, 1999
HOW WARS END

CRAZY HORSE is killed, betrayed by a brother. Chief Joseph has said he will fight no more forever. Sitting Bull has become a carnie. Severed buffalo heads putrify naked plains once furred with grasses bejeweled with waterbeads. The people are whipped and sick, huddled in cages, and then one winter day in 1889 during a total eclipse of the sun, a man, name of Wovoka, a.k.a. Jack, has a vision of divine renewal, and one summer day in 1999, a man, name of Henry, humps his carry-on through the wide white corridors of the Atlanta airport and emerges into a sickly hot morning and looks up and down the line of double parked cars and has a vision of Her leaning against the side of a red BMW. Wearing a long, loose, Indonesian print dress. Wearing the brown shoes with the straps. Orange nail polish on the toes. Jaw. Red ringlet mane. Mother-of-pearl necklace that not many women could wear set against that throat so smooth so…

Go to Her.

These encountering moments. Will they hug? Will they kiss? Will it be cheek or lips? Will She say something that alters everything, and will it be of the Lucy-yanking-the-football-away-from-Charlie-Brown's-foot variety or of the baby-here's-everything-you-ever-wanted school?

They hug. Nothing else, though perhaps something else would have followed it if the traffic cop, who'd been perfectly patient when She was leaning there alone, didn't walk behind the car with pen and pad, prodding Her, perhaps, to break the somewhat motherly clasp in which She held Henry—at this point not a word has been spoken. She pops the trunk with a handheld remote prompting Henry to toss in his carry-on and slide in the passenger side.

"How are you?"

"Good."

Vroom.

"How are you?"

"Good."

Urrrrrch!

She's a fiend. Henry grips the handstrap. He's thinking he didn't realize Atlanta had freeways like California but Atlanta does. He's thinking he doesn't know what to take away from that hug, the coolness of it, the withholding; that familiar opening move of Hers that always lays our boy low, though now, accompanying the lowering, he experiences a bracing jolt of anger and thinks: can't She say hello without lunging for the upper hand? He thinks: have I ever seen this play before? He thinks: Henry, you petty prick—focus not on power plays but on love, on your responsibility to touch something, something divine, for the Conquistador, for yourself, for your beloved. He thinks: stop thinking! And finally: here beside me—thank you God—here She is.

"Nice car."

"It's my sister's."

"Nice sister."

"You'll meet her."

"When?"

"After you meet my mom."

"When do I meet your mom?"

"Before you meet my dad."

"Is there a proper order?"

"My mom comes first."

"Your dress is lovely."

"Thank you."

"It's more grown up than I'm used to with you."

"You mean less sexy?"

"Mature."

"Less sexy."

"So I'm meeting your family."

"I hope that's O.K.."

"You hope…"

A fishtail off the freeway, onto wide surface streets. She slows markedly. Big wooden houses with bygone grace. Oaks and willows, elegant vines and puckered blossoms. French doors opening onto second-floor porches. Gardens. Sheds. Swings.

A man raking grass.

A red BMW buoyed by Her smile.

A wrinkle: *I hope that's O.K.*

A wary, schizophrenic, messianic, boy.

In Wovoka's vision, the earth opens, the enemy is swallowed, the people are lifted to safety by thunderbirds and deposited back down to a world of roaming buffalo and plains regrassed and rejeweled and all the people, the living and the dead, arrive in this place happy and young. All the lovers arrive. All the mothers and fathers and sisters, the babies born and unborn. All together. But first…

Arrive the mother.

She lives in a single-story brick house that she's lived in for thirty years. It is surrounded by exactly twenty-two pines. The needles have all been herded into piles and between the piles, grass grows thinly, stiffened and split by furious raking and caked in dust. Here and there, chicken wire rings freshly planted flowers, yellow and purple agapanthus—all caked, as well, in dust. Brown vines cling like lizards to red brick, and Henry stares at these lizards, he even takes a step back and shrinks, for he sees this place for what it is—graceless, worked to the bone. And then he abruptly turns, encounters Her smile and the dust and lizards are gone, replaced by buffalo and bejeweled grasses and all the people happy and together.

A newly poured cement pathway leads from the BMW to the thin screen door. The mother opens it. She's got her daughter's mouth. She hugs her daughter and gleefully protests the kisses.

"Mom, this is Henry."

The thin screen door snaps shut. Mother and daughter are inside. Henry is…

"Mom!"

Arrive the father. The face made for staring down fish. The homeless schizophrenic who lives in his Jeep. The culprit. The source. (Though her move to California cut off the supply of pancakes served surreptitiously in Her mother's driveway, She continued a low-profile long-distance relationship with Her father via collect calls from him to Her on pay phones).

They meet at a haunt of his, a lowball family restaurant that takes its cue from Denny's. He slides into the booth across from them. With Her arm and Her head and Her lips, She's acting more than girlfriendy, She's acting like Henry and She have spent months in private steadily building a sound institution and are now ready to take it public.

"Dad, this is Henry."

Dad's hand stabs across the table, and Henry takes it but dad's not looking at Henry, he's looking at his own hand, as if startled, and then annoyed, by its uppity act of social grace.

"Nice to meet you."

Dad nods.

They order biscuits and gravy, all of them. Henry asks for an extra egg. Dad's thin black hair is restroom-slicked and his teeth are few, but his table manners remain intact; no gravy befouls that big-rig jaw.

Her jaw, Henry thinks. Mister Half-Fucking-Cherokee. The madman who made Her what She is.

Henry has expected to feel hatred for this man, but none

comes. Henry's prepared himself to be fascinated by Dad's face, that origin of the infection. But Henry's vision, at this point, is filtered through a messianic cloth, and to be fair, Dad, in this moment, inspires neither hatred nor fascination. Dad's a child trying to act in a way he thinks people, in these situations, act. He talks of the theater, of which Henry knows nothing. Sensing this, She asks Her father to sing a show tune with her. Instead, he's off on Civil War trivia. Bull Run. Antietam. Why this officer was canned, the total number of casualties under his unfortunate command, the caliber and weight of guns. She leans Her head on Henry's shoulder. She fixes Her father with smile. He's on to Jefferson Davis, Reconstruction, the number of lynchings in a Georgia county in one month. Without removing the smile, the attentive gaze, from Her father, She nuzzles Henry's neck. It shoots him through with quivers.

Dad speaks of the legendary leader of a thieving, murdering band of holdouts. "Mmm," She purrs, into Henry's neck. Stabbed in the back by his own men, who'd grown tired of fighting, who'd decided to take the government up on its offer of full amnesty only to be mowed down by Gatling guns after reciting the Pledge of Allegiance in a Union camp.

"It could have been him," She says, "the leader, who stabbed them in the back."

"The specifics of who exactly is behind this thing," he says, "would bring down several counties of this state, and two in another."

She lifts Her head from Henry's shoulder. Her smile slips off. "What other?" She says.

He drags his fork across the plate, lifting the last of the gravy. He sucks the tines. He touches his unblemished chin with his napkin and Henry thinks: Look at this. Listen to what these people are saying. Their logic is frightening. These people, they're mad.

"Good," Dad says. His eyes lock onto his daughters', and he begins to sing. It's a show tune. *Tomorrow, tomorrow.* The theme from Annie. About believing in hope, in joy, in spite of everything. She joins her father in song. They serenade one another, loudly, complete with sweeping arm gestures and faraway looks and coquettish tips of the head and patrons are staring and the manager is staring and Henry realizes She and Her father must have sung it together a thousand times and every time just like this time and every time they become, like this sillysappy song, gorgeous, clearly in love, and every time the black-lava demons glare down from their striated shoulders, Her father's and Hers.

The tune ends. She presses Her lips to Henry's neck. "Mmm," She says, and the sound dribbles down his spine, licking at bone and nerve, eating away until there's no more wariness or schizophrenia— no more Henry. There's just this warm puddle of sauce.

Arrive the sister's condominium complex. It's in a neighborhood of condominium complexes, fitness centers and convenience stores. She comes home from work in a business suit. Henry and Her are already there, sitting at a the round plastic table in the eat-in kitchen. The sister drops a fat clump of keys on the table, drapes the suit jacket over a chair, glowers down at Henry.

"I guess you think you're better," says the sister.

Henry wonders how this stranger knows anything about the Conquistador and his religion of better, then realizes she means the fiancé.

"I guess so," says Henry, side-eyeing Her to gauge Her reaction but there is none. She's surveying the contents of the closed white refrigerator with X-ray eyes. While dignity demands he return the sister's stern negotiator's gaze, dignity also permits his thoughts to sample goodies like these: if She hadn't smashed Her face and had Her nose reconstructed, this nose, Her sister's cauliflower nose, would have been Hers; the sister believes She is not living right by God; the sister has refused to have contact with the father for years; as children sleeping in the same bed, She would entwine Her limbs around the sister and the sister would disentangle herself and go crying to the mother; as children, She shot the sister in the ass with a BB gun and laughed through the spanking.

Arrive the evening. An upscale downtown bar/restaurant specializing in oysters trucked up from Louisiana and white wines flown over from California. White tablecloths and a pearl-white bar edged in stainless steel. The light is uniform and bright. It bejewels the fruits of the sea—gray oyster shells, red crayfish (where Henry's from they call them crayfish), white rings of marinated squid. Outside, a muggy dusk has a half-hour wait. Inside, the place is packed with New South suits. Henry's pressed into an alcove by the window. He's sipping a Chardonnay. He's sitting on a stool with his feet on the one She just vacated with a kiss and a whisper of be right back. He's thinking about the day, the disturbing enchanting procession of kin. He's likening it to being escorted under a white flag behind enemy lines by an officer in an uniform impossible to peg as one side's or the other's. He's thinking: Is this an armistice or just a brief break in the action? Do these people love me or want to see me dead? Who's the enemy? Is there an enemy? Can wars simply end in togetherness and love? Perhaps yes, perhaps all it takes is a leap of faith, perhaps…

She places a bundle of flowers on the narrow counter next to him, climbs onto Her stool, hikes up the Indonesian dress, and entwines those hardhoney legs in his.

"Someone called and said to go pick up these flowers," She says. She does a mane dip in the direction of the street. "Up the street there."

Henry studies the passers by. "Someone sent you flowers, huh?"

"There's a card."

"Open it."

"No, you."

The restaurant's bright lights are doing the same thing to Her mouth as they are to the fruits of the sea. Only now there's no shell, just the softness inside, the sparkle of spit. But he does not like the idea that someone sent Her flowers, so he does not obey the imperative; he does not kiss Her.

God he wants to kiss Her.

"Open it," She says.

He does, and a little two-by-two card with an agapanthus imprinted on its front.

"Read it," She says, and places Her hands on his thighs, and lowers Her head so Her mane rakes his zipper. "Out loud."

"Dear Henry and (Her)," he reads, "Can't wait to see you both around February Sixteenth. Your greatest fan."

He lowers the card.

"It's from our baby," She says.

He stares into the suits.

"I've been so alone," She says to his chest.

The suits assume the glittering, sculpted form of a frieze. It's dazzling. This frieze, these figures, coated in crystal as if they'd been lifted from the sea.

"Henry, say something."

Dazzling in their sea crystal, dazzling vision of the glittering risen, dazzling…sea.

He cups Her jaw in his hands, lifts Her, touches Her tears, speaks into Her mouth. "You're not alone anymore."

Arrive the imperative, and obey.

From cages across the land, emissaries of the whipped and the sick and of the poor defeated people are sent to visit the prophet, and emissaries return to their cages with the miraculous news and the people say yes, God yes, how do we get there? And the answer is: conduct yourselves in a morally upright fashion. And the answer is: dance. Or rather, Ghost Dance. More specifically, do this dance for five nights and four days and the dead will rise, the grasses will thrive, the enemy will vanish into the earth. And the people, the poor desperate people, they do the Ghost Dance like there's no tomorrow and the enemy, the victorious enemy, they hear of this and become concerned and begin mobilizing troops, which the people don't see so hell-bent they are, so blinded by misery and hope. In this state, the people see only love, only beauty. In this state, they see only the world they've longed for all their lives. The world as it should be. The world of Henry and Her and their embryo of love together forever and ever. In Atlanta. In a B&B *né* mansion of a Civil War general.

She's got it all booked, already (the tab goes to the Glamrag).

The place is set back from the treecalmed street by a seagreen lawn. A sprinkler bejewels the thriving blades. A curving white porch is sanctuaried from view by a hanging garden, a Borneo of vine and bud. They mount the stairs to the porch, pass beyond the savage flora and find a porch swing awaiting. She smiles, touches him, guides him inside, and the dining room's dark oak is riven by a limber dusk-sun through which they pass bewitched by dust angels. Touching, they ascend the stairway to the second floor, and the house resounds with sounds greater than them, greater than now. In their bedroom, lined with classics, She throws open the French doors (yes, like the Lighthouse, God rest its soul) and strides onto their second-floor porch. He stands at the foot of their four-poster affair, gazing upward, at the blue lording down through the stained glass window, the blue lording the bed.

Her hands thrill his hips.

He turns. He takes Her hands in his fingertips. He guides Her with a touch gentle as a nod. She eases Herself against the quilt. She's on her back, feet lolling off the foot of the bed, and he bends and unclasps the straps of a lovely brown shoe. He places it soundlessly on the floor. Looks along the length of Her. Smiles. Unclasps the other. Lays it against its mate. Carefully furls the big dress over calves, knees, thighs, belly, and look, see the lord-blue swell, bellyswell no longer snake-taut but rounded now, full and filling you must kiss me, us, family of you.

"Kiss me there," She says.

She says, "Feel how heavy my breasts are?"

"Baby," She says, "we're home."

This vision of Home, it's so real it reeks. Pepper of oaks, yeast of grass, salt of flowers. Bees churn, blending the scents. The sun is a woman whose hot and moist and honeylusty skin one can't help but brush against everywhere. Streets are jungle rivers. Porches doorless, windowless dwellings. Ice cream taunts. Leather beckons. A barbershop caters to blacks. For the cultural pleasure of it, She has

Her hair done there in a two-hour affair complete with tin foil and an overhead dryer and glass-fronted photos of pomaded luminaries and a wiry stylist twisting around Her chair pointing out his favorite do's in the magazine through which She serenely leafs while he, Henry, pretends to nap, trying to hide his smile.

A secondhand clothing store not unlike the one where She bought the breakaway skirt and monster truck boots only this time She's with Her man Henry and they're hunting for pregnant lady clothes. As it turns out, the slip-dressed salesgirl's a mother herself, she's got the pictures to prove it.

She: "He's beautiful."

Salesgirl: "He's wonderful."

"Father around?"

"Dad loves him."

"That's great."

"Yeah."

"He. . .?"

"Dad's no deadbeat. First of the month. On time every time. "

Mane dip and lift. "Girl, you got it goin' on."

"Shit."

They laugh and disappear amongst the racks. Henry hears murmuring. More laughter. The salesgirl's voice: "You'll grow out of that in a month." Hers: "Oh my God it's huge." Salesgirl: "Believe me." Her: "Oh God."

Henry ambles over to the disheveled rack of shoes. He's got some notion of trying something on, but he can't tell the difference between men's and women's, so he touches neither until She appears in something approximating a muumuu and it's true, She can indeed puddle him in a muumuu, so much so that he tries on and parades around in a pair of women's shoes.

She asks him to walk past Her and the salesgirl one more time.

"My boo's wearin' shoes."

"Yo boo's a fine figure of a shoe wearin' man."

"Fine figure of a daddy."

"Y'all...?

"Haven't gotten there."

"No rush."

"Mmm."

After all the puddling and parading, he still can't bring himself to purchase unmanly shoes. In the teeth of Her sulk, he returns them to the rack and hauls on his bad old boots. The salesgirl tsk-tsks. The women hug like parting kin. "You'll be so happy," the salesgirl says huskily. "Both of you will I promise."

Standing by the door, Henry looks on as a tear tickles the corner of his eye. He smiles. His mind is calm. His thoughts are pure. He thinks: finally, I'm winning.

A restaurant in the woods on the edge of town. A World War II theme of the heavy machinery variety. A tank guards the long and winding driveway's entrance. On the grass out back the restaurant: bombers. Beyond the bombers, golfers stroke through the day's final light. The line dividing gunner from duffer is imperceptible. At least it is to Henry, who finds this messiness unsettling. He turns from the window, looks directly at the mother. Because she's speaking directly to him.

"You two have not been responsible."

"No." Henry shakes his head.

"Now you must start."

"Yes." Henry nods.

"Yes. So. What are your plans?"

"Mom, he just got here," She says. "We haven't had a chance really to talk."

"Well, I'd suggest you start," says the mother.

"Yes," says Henry. "We will."

He eats a massive pepper steak, and the three of them retire to the veranda out back of the restaurant. Some sort of nick-of-time wedding party's going on, or it's a pudgy reunion of fraternity brothers and their spouses. Lite beer and coolers all around. She, Henry, and the mother perch on a round waterless fountain set in flagstones. Above them, moths adore a tin-backed light. Low to the ground hunt the mosquitoes. She slaps at Her thigh, stands and crosses to the grassy edge of illumination, paces it. Henry and the mother sit watching Her taut patrol. Far and away, heat lightning; Henry squints into the night; the duffers, it seems, have all taken cover but the bombers remain, dark shapes now, dynamic absences.

And He thinks: whumpsuck. He thinks: three black helicopters flying in formation and even the sun can't resist; even the sun, in the presence of this absence, flutters and fades. He thinks: this rumble in my belly, is it thunderbirds coming to bear me above the flood or the sound of galloping cavalry hooves? He thinks: thank God I'll never be Out There again.

Later, they drive to the mother's house and eat green ice cream, and She lays on the couch with Her head in Henry's lap while the mother talks of the Century Foundation, how the three back-to-back sixteen-hour days spent defeating her fears in a room with more than two hundred other people defeating theirs have increased her "impactiveness" a thousandfold. Later still, the two of them drive back to the general's mansion, and he asks if She'd consider doing the Century Foundation's three-day seminar, and She says, in light of the wonders it's done for Her mother, She wouldn't rule it out, which unsettles Henry enough that as they're nearing their destination, he outs with another question that's been nagging at him but that he's been too chickenshit, too loathe to play the role of killjoy to his own unfolding paradise, to ask.

"Are you…I guess you are...you know that, um, it's, mine."

Vroom! Urrch!

Two hours of the silent treatment for Henry.

Afterwards, in bed, She patiently explains that She did not have sex with the fiancé after New Mexico and only once before, which took place on the night She arrived in New Orleans from California ("He threw a surprise party for me. Fucking disaster."), and that a woman doctor had professionally pinned the conception on the lit chiles.

"I'm sorry," says Henry, and he means this more than She can know, more than he himself ever knew until now, until becoming the morally upright Ghost Dancer that he is; he means I'm sorry, oh

God, for doubting you; I'm sorry for the Goddess, for my faithless notions of love as a hangnail; I'm sorry for my cowardice in the face of the monsters and wonk, sorry for Valentino, for vanity. He means *Hear me, oh Lord, hear me vow that from this day on I will walk in a manner that forever makes You proud.*

"Baby," She says, nuzzling Her cheek into his chest. "you know my mom's right, we do need to talk about what we're going to do."

He kisses Her temple. "We're going to be together forever."

December, 1890. A frozen plain called Wounded Knee. A band of desperate believers clad in Ghost Shirts. Painted onto them are sacred symbols, turtles and thunderbirds, which render the wearer impervious to bullets. Closing in on the believers is a fearsome contingent of enemy troops. Of edgy conscripts. It's dark and early. Five a.m. to be exact. In the general's mansion, the morning after the bomber restaurant, She wakes him at five. She's already showered and dressed.

"Get up," She says. "We're going to the clinic."

"What's the matter? What's wrong?"

"I'm having an abortion."

"But—."

"Let's go."

"No."

"I'm sorry."

"But—."

"Would you prefer I went through this alone?"

He drives and She navigates from a pamphlet printed on recycled paper. On its cover is a silhouette drawing of a Rubenesque female, smiling. She's got the overhead lamp on, studying the pamphlet's hand drawn map. "Two more blocks and right on Peach Street." They enter a neighborhood with big wooden houses with grace long gone. A Delta 88 hiked up on blocks. A rusty red bicycle with a warped wheel locked to a porch rail. Wretched lawns. "It's up ahead, on the left." She switches off the lamp. No need for it now anyhow.

The world is swaddled in execution light, and Henry wonders why someone once deemed this the appropriate hour to end things.

Henry wonders, this is true, but it's an abstract business like wondering how Vikings got their name. He doesn't believe this execution will go through any more than he believes Vikings will swoop down the streets of Atlanta. He fears not. He believes, one might say, in the power of the ghost shirt.

A green-vested "escort" walks them through the gauntlet of protesters and their pictures.

Inside, a woman opens her sliding window. Into her huge hand, Henry places his Amex (will the Glamrag tab this?). She fits the card into the manual mechanism, lifts the black metal arm, slams home the payment. Crackthud. A primitive mechanism, but they're hers now.

In the waiting room, there's no men and a surprising calm. The women whisper and giggle. Toddlers sprawl on the floor. A fat woman nurses a tiny baby. Many have been here before, many will be back. This too, they seem to say to Henry, shall pass.

In the midst She and Henry sit. They've been touching in some form or another since they paid. Now the fingers of all four hands entwine. Her mane is a place of refuge. A lot of kissing goes on in there. Rubbing of wet faces. Talk profoundly at odds with the event of the moment. And yet both Henry and Her quicken to the rhetoric.

"I want to have your baby."

"I want you to have my baby."

They call Her and take Her. Henry leafs through a magazine he cannot read—he cannot make out the words. The women in the waiting room drone like priests. It is a stop-time sound, a forever pause. It's like light in the Dark Woods. It's a sound to curl up in, and Henry does, he closes his eyes, and stares into the fire.

"Baby. Baby!"

Henry opens his eyes.

"We have to go to the window."

He follows, his mind still folded in on itself like a salted slug.

"Give her your credit card."

He does, his faculties now beginning to flex, and he braces for the expected pain while also sensing the presence of something unexpected; something not…pain.

The woman runs the card through the mechanism. Crackthud. Only different this time. The woman hands Henry a credit slip.

"The thirty dollars," she says, "goes to processing."

Henry looks at the slip. Two hundred and fifty dollars. He looks at the school clock above the window. Seven oh five. That's twenty minutes. She was in there only twenty minutes.

They go outside. Down an alley. He halts Her in a metal doorway. Hot and bright with sun. Corners puddled with trash. Henry in the usual, the Converse All Star t-shirt. Henry in an idiot grin, struck silly by the power of belief. Henry in the wake of a miracle that he made happen. Swaddled in hallelujah light. With the Conquistador's voice, gruff and choked, in his ear, saying: No affront to God now. Oh ho no! You're an honor to all of us. Faith— Fuck, Henry! Feature of a goddamn man.

And still—Fuck, Henry!—he still can't help asking. "You didn't…?"

The doorway resonates with smile. "No silly," She says. "I didn't."

That night, they go to the nightclub district and stroll right down the middle of the streets with all the other revelers and She tells him, in that casual way, about the sonogram the nurse made Her look at while Henry was waiting with the priests, about the sonogram that showed "the world's most perfect fist," and then She shifts, in that casual way, to stories of how She used to be in this place, of cruising in teenage girl-packs and the girls peeling off one by one with strangers and not even lying to mama because mama couldn't do a thing about it.

"I was a wild child," She says.

They're on the dotted yellow line and still, the street is packed. A woman is walking straight at Henry with her arms outstretched. Henry's woman's breath catches, and Henry is pulled toward Her and the woman passes and hugs a total stranger.

She breathes, clinging to him. "I thought you knew her."

She's still clinging to him in bed as their exhausted bodies give way, and in the morning, as they wake, and at the airport gate, a few minutes before the final boarding call, he's thinking he should say something. He's thinking they've said nothing of consequence since the clinic. He's thinking: faith. He asks Her when She's planning on joining him and She says a week, maybe two, She doesn't know, She's got an open ticket, She needs to spend time with Her family, She'll call. Final call. Hug and kiss. Gimme another. Shoulder bag. Pause and turn.

I love you.

I love you.

A massacre in the snow, and rise.

Rise and gaze down upon blue-coated soldiers still milling, still quivering. On the bodies of women and children, on the men with their bloody ghost shirts that clearly don't work, on the red-on-white. Down there: the imprint of an eagle in a soldier's brass button. On a squaw's bloodless hand, the third finger has been hacked off at the joint. It's a ritual of grief—a loved one has died. And not ten feet from the squaw's finger and no bigger than her hand, the loved one. Henry's embryo. Due January Sixteenth. Henry's greatest fan, balled in the snow. A blue marble on the plain. Does death feel like this— like rising and gazing down? Gazing down upon death? From a place not of darkness but of immeasurable light, immeasurable heat.

Are Henry's embryo's little digits still grasping at ice crystals?

No matter. The squaw's finger has already been hacked. And even if it was still intact, there's nothing Henry can do. For he doesn't know. He boards the plane in Atlanta and disembarks in the fog at SFO. He takes the shuttle to the Irish bar ("Open 6 a.m.!") where the Conquistador waits with Henry's underpowered pickup and the pre-agreed keys to Henry's slick new charity port one point three miles up the sidewinder, and they seethe, seethe through gravel to the Glamshack while mom, in the brick house in Atlanta, brings Her tea. Mom brings Her pork chops and green ice cream. Mom smoothes Her mane and talks of sleep schedules and day care and budgets. Mom offers Her and Henry a room in her house until they get on their feet. Mom dabs at Her tears. Mom says, Does he love you? Does he want you? Are you sure? Mom suggests the Century Foundation—so She can be sure. (Was it mom's idea, the Century Foundation, or was it Hers?) Mom shuttles Her to and from the three-day seminar. The thousandfold increase in "impactiveness," the elation of power, the delirium of certainty: no, She is not convinced beyond a shadow of a doubt that Henry cannot live without Her, that he will not go on without Her, and in light of that threat She must protect Herself, She must ensure Her own survival; so yes, She is sure.

Mom behind the wheel of a pristine Dodge Dart and mom's handing her credit card to the woman with the huge hand and mom waits with the priests and lends a shoulder on the walk to the car and drives Her home and puts Her to bed and a week later sees Her off at the gate and in six hours, Henry picks Her up in the fog at SFO and shuttles Her to the sunny Glamshack ("Isn't it slick?" "Totally slick.") and She tells him about her mother and the Century Foundation and the abortion, all of it at once, matter-of-factly, as if the abortion was something unpleasant that had to be done, everyone would agree it had to be done, and it was done. She had it done, believe it or not, and believe it he does not. Or rather: he hears the gunfire and does not see the bodies in the snow.

He sees only Her, that She's with him, that he's so relieved to have Her with him that all is forgiven in the spirit of starting fresh, in the remnants of the spirit of divine renewal, and they pick grasses, all of them different, and put them in a plastic cup in the bedroom and make love and pie and then She announces that She is leaving for twelve days to visit the fiancé ("I have to do this. So I won't regret."), and Her leaving is heralded by mangling gravel, the whumpsuck of black helicopters, and Her absence ignites a fevered trek back to the Mumbletypeg days, on up through Enchanted Moments, the War, the

Lightness, the Goddess, the Fiancé, and the Bloom, pauses briefly in these everhotter woods, skulks around the madman, around and around, demands continuously of Self and God in everlouder tones *how did this happen? How could you let this happen? How can you stop this happening? How could you be falling deeper in love with Her when the goal of this evil conjuring and reliving is escape? How could you love a woman who would rather kill that little embryo of love than live with the sliver of possibility that you are not utterly, pathetically dependent on Her, that you might go on without Her? Is this the woman who placed a flower on your table in the cafe, who shared with the madman the power of all possibility, whose presence, like the madman's, infuses a man with mystery, divinity? Are you truly one with the dead now? Are you finally free? After terrible battles, after one great last hope, after rising above the bloody ghost shirts, the cold blue marble, a divine shine, a divine heat, is this really how wars end—with fire in the eyes and sun in the throat?*

AUGUST 20, 1999
GLAMSHACK

I HEAR HER. I'm sitting on my porch, drinking my morning coffee, squinting through the sun at a hummingbird hovering so golden green, like a pixie, and I hear the bleat of babydoll rap. Coming from the road below. The music winds in and out of earshot with each forested curve, and each curve cranks it louder. Then She strikes gravel, and the rushclatter beneath the bleating drives the hummingbird away; or rather, it wisely fades. She must have the top down because the white top never appears above the weeds and I feel so sad for them, the brown weeds. They're weak in this parched heat. A passing car, a breeze and—see: one just came tumbling down.

She turns onto my spur and stops and the gravel seethes up short like a river coming to rest and I think: my house, the end; a river.

She approaches the porch by way of the pool's lip. In the brown shoes. She does a little balance beam routine and there's nothing unusual in this, nothing unusual at all. So profoundly usual is this image of Her return that I wonder if it's real, if I'm not doing a bit of New Orleans-style conjuring. And then I see the cigarette. As She balance-beams, She holds between Her fingers the last of a lit cigarette and I've never seen Her smoke. I would not have conjured Her smoking. So I am not conjuring Her. Nor am I conjuring this fear of fire—in these woods, it's been hot and dry for an eternity, and here She is, smoking a fucking cigarette.

She pauses at the porch steps, grinds out the cigarette on the base of Her brown shoe.

"That's a feat," I say.

She cocks her head. "You've seen me balance before, baby."

"The cigarette."

Her lip quivers, and I notice there's no sore, and suddenly there's a talon in my chest.

"I don't really smoke," She says.

"In a convertible. I mean smoking a cigarette in a convertible."

She does a mane dip and lift and the smile that She unwinds, the python I know so well, it coils around my neck and constricts.

She says, "Actually, it's easy."

I say, "Do you want some coffee?"

And I'm in the kitchen pouring coffee. Strong and black, the way I like it. And there's no half and half for Her to make it creamy, the way She likes it. Time was I would have made damn sure to get a fresh one but this time it didn't cross my mind. The house, too, is unprepared. Indian Wars book open on the floor. Wine in a wine glass on the counter. A wooden chair in the middle of the room. I've been so hell-bent on thinking about Her these past twelve days that I haven't considered Her. Her taste, Her skin. Even now, with Her out there on my porch anticipating creamy coffee only it won't be creamy, it will be strong and black instead—even now I can't quite envision Her body. Or rather: I can't envision it whole.

I return to the porch and there She is sitting on the boards with Her legs outstretched and Her bare arms buttressed behind Her and I hand Her the coffee and sit in my chair and She sips and swallows and does not say a word.

Nor do I. For the first time, I see what She's wearing. The blue dress I bought for Her at the beach. The dress that yanked stares from passersby. It's tight and short. It shows a lot of body, this dress, this body that I want so bad but I can't see it. I see a brown blotch on the front of the right calf. I see veins on the back of Her right hand. The third toe on her left foot, it is orange. Which means they must all be orange. They are. She sips Her coffee and Her mane sways and Her jaw dips. And I feel I could be looking at anyone's jaw. So I look for pores, in Her face that could only be Hers. I find one. Large and dark, like I remember. Larger and darker than I remember. I don't remember them so large and dark. Perhaps that's on account of the sun berrying the skin around it. Perhaps this could be anyone's pore. It bears no relation to any other part of Her body. Her breasts, look at Her breasts, I know those breasts, the sunblush, the purple nipples hard and pressing, the other animal they suggest, the otherness of all of this: pore, tit, jaw that could be anyone's. These disassembled features, it's like that humble-craftsman-piece-of-shit Raynard said of women in his nightmare-funny Roman ruin—they could be anyone. She…could be.

She's smoking another cigarette. I watch Her go to grind it out in an abalone shell. I see Her no-nonsense hand dip into the mother-of-pearl necklace and pause and I hear Her ask if I mind and I hear myself say no. I've got them lying all over the place. I'm waiting for the ants to clean them but you know they're so rich around here they don't have ants ha-ha and She smiles and says it's probably too hot and dry for them and I agree, it's hotter than anything I've ever seen. She asks if She may have one, a shell, to send to the Indian woman in New Mexico who made the necklace, so that she can make more necklaces and more women can feel as beautiful and special as She does when She wears it. She smiles up at me, from the planks. She's bending toward Her feet and the cleavage deepens and the blue dress rides up the hardhoney thigh and the brown shoes unclasp and lift off the feet and come to rest mate against mate on the planks and one foot cracks and orange toes point and the big one draws, and draws again: S.

Special. She says this. Even without the mother-of-pearl necklace, She can't remember where She left it, don't worry She'll remember, do I remember, I must remember, the chiles, the bed.

And quietly, She smiles and leans to Her left and lifts, between two tensed palms, an abalone shell. She lifts it to Her head, and as She does, sun sparks the shell's brilliant belly, and still smiling quietly, She holds it above Her head, and sun sparks throughout Her mane, and then She sits up straight and asks what She looks like and I don't answer and She says, "An Aztec queen in a Conquistador's helmet. Isn't that strange?"

I agree: it's strange.

She feels, She says, so strange. So special. She will always remember this special feeling between us. No matter what happens. No matter how I respond. To what She's come to say. Or rather: to the message She's come to deliver.

And the eagle's talons pierce my chest anew, and the python ratchets down another notch, and I reach for something to push Her away—the embryo of love. The little dead embryo. The embryo She erased to ensure Her supremacy. The murderess, right there on the planks. I love a murderess. Her foot cracks. She's come to say something. To deliver. She tugs downward on Her blue dress. She smiles. Quickly in the lips.

"I'm marrying him," She says. "I'm marrying my fiancé."

"No."

"Yes."

"When?"

"A month."

"You can't."

"I must."

"I love you"

"I love you too, Henry," She says. "But if I don't marry him, I'll die."

"But…"

"It's O.K. baby," She says. "It's gonna be O.K.." And then She explains that She called the Glamrag looking for Henry and got Roland and they talked of Henry, of how much they loved him, of his depth and beauty, of his foolish lovely suffering, of what Roland called Henry's hero's fate and how Roland shared that fate but really, the thing that sealed the deal for Her was when Roland placed upon her head the Conquistador's helmet.

"I know you called him," says Henry. "I didn't know you met him."

"The man's a force. I know you know this. I couldn't not meet him."

"Where?"

"His office."

"What time? says Henry. "Morning? Evening? Was anybody else there?"

She draws on the brown shoes and clasps the straps. The berry in Her face has blanched. Her soreless lips quiver, and She says given all the knuckleballs She's hurled Henry's way She doesn't blame him for thinking She fucked Roland in his office and truth be told there was a time in Her life, which is to say most of the adult part and some of the child, when She would have fucked him in his office just as She'd fucked countless men in offices (or not offices) but thanks to Henry, who restored Her power to love, She never considered fucking Roland in his office, though he did consider fucking Her.

"How do you know?"

"I know."

And She stands, lights another cigarette, walks past the pool, no balance-beaming now. She gets in Her car and dangles a lit cigarette out the window, and I see orange sparks and the little spiral dance She does with Her smoky fingers, which I assume is meant for me, and I think: Before you destroy everything, please put it out. Then I hear the sound of the engine and the bleat of the music and the river that landed Her at the Glamshack begins again backwards.

But instead of turning downhill, the way She came, She drives to the end of my gravel and turns up. Up from my house, there are only two more houses beyond which no one lives, and there are very few oaks. There are redwoods, the forest of which has more grandeur than the Dark Woods, and more darkness. I've been up there only twice. Once alone, lost on a fast run. Once with Her, to pick grasses, all of them different, which we placed in a plastic cup in my bedroom, and my chest gives a great heave—She remembered, She didn't forget. I'm sitting on my porch looking up there and it's like peering through a sea, a heaving sea, a sea so violent I'm not sure what I see but I can't stop looking. I sit. I sense the sun ascend above this heaving (belly) sea. I sense the sweat of hours. And then, finally, I see.

Her and Roland. Together in the wide-open area at the Glamrag that's studded with tables covered in clippings. It's near dark. Is there a table between them? There is. The Conquistador's talking about his life before the betrayal by Jonathon Smart and the further betrayal by Johnnie Walker. Before the film ground down. When the grand man walked with his huntress. When he breathed sun. Dancing atop those bloody swords. Grand, damned man. And they talked about Her, the blessed demons She inherited from her father. And they talked about love, Henry's and Hers, how gorgeous it was, and bloodied by the fact of the fiancé. And as they talked of blessed damnation and bloodied love, the Conquistador's craving surged. The thing he needed to breathe, here it was standing across the table. He couldn't breathe. He kept talking. And then he stopped. And stared at the Glamrag's frayed carpet. Comprehending. And She says, "Are you there?"

"Yes."

"Are you O.K.?"

"Hmm."

"You understand."

"I do."

"I can't tell you how that makes me feel. To know there's someone out there who knows how I feel. How Henry feels. How we do."

He says, "I know."

She says, "I talk to you, I feel like I'm talking to Henry."

"I know."

"I should leave."

"No."

"What then?"

"Come."

"Where?"

"My office. I want to give you something."

She does a mane dip and follows him through the large, dark room. A panther, a predator, She moves easily between the scrap-covered tables, around jutting corners. Her hips shy from the point of a scissors, but She does not break stride. To the one frosted glass door lit from within. They enter. He walks to the bookshelf and reaches behind the stacks of scripts and takes down the helmet and holds it out, weeping, for all that torments him, and an unnoticed Glamrag staffer (the sexy-chubby blond!) douses the last light and boards the elevator and the Conquistador's bids Her sit in his chair but She'd prefer to stand. So they stand. She in the brown shoes and jeans and the shirt that throws Her chest into relief and the mother-of-pearl necklace, the one that not many women could wear, and he in a musty, finely tailored suit.

Her bearing is regal. Her feet flex. Her breasts are as taut as Her belly and Her jaw, Her hair glimmers in the fluorescence, and She says something about Henry, and as She says it, She fills the room with smile. And the Conquistador breathes, for the first time in many, many years, sun.

And he feels powerless. And he's so sorry. He is truly sorry. For a man does not do what he's about to do to another man. A compadre. But does anyone know how long it's been since he stood in this presence? Breathed it? Gorged? Does anyone know how it feels to live without God?

God, he thinks, I am so sorry.

And he reaches to the top of the bookshelf, behind the brittle film scripts, and brings down the helmet, and as if She knew this would happen, in the middle of the tiny room, She stops, quivering, and he lifts the helmet between two rigid palms to Her head.

"Do you know what you look like?" he asks.

She smiles.

"You look," he says, "like an Aztec queen in a Conquistador's helmet."

She does not move.

"You are the union of powerful, opposing forces."

Nary a muscle.

"You are beautiful."

Her smile disappears.

"This is yours."

He is Hers. And yet for the first time in Her life, She does not take possession. Because, just as being watched no longer feeds Henry, possessing no longer suckles Her. Because She understands that by losing everything—the film, the woman, God—the Conquistador has done what he set out to do: he has come down from the mountain and breathed sun down all our bitten throats. And this understanding thrills Her in a way owning and manipulating bodies and parts of bodies never has, and also kills Her, and She knows now that Her own damned grandeur resides with the fiancé. Or rather, with his happiness. Henry is Her love, but the fiancé is Her fate; by giving up Henry—by offering up the joy he'd restored in Her soul—She might redress the wrong She committed against the fiancé; She might rekindle joy in him. And who knows? Maybe once that happened he'd move on, leaving Her free to be with Henry. Maybe She'd be eighty when this happened, Her flesh fallen and Henry's too, the act of love no longer an entranced prayer performed deep inside one another's gleaming earthly temples but something sad, sweet, felt not in the flesh but in the bones, something She'd never before this numinous moment imagined.

She will do this. She will squirrel away this vision of Henry and Her together at eighty, and She will do this.

So She gives the Conquistador a warm kiss on the lips and shows Herself out. The outer door clicks, and he feels the balm of relief and also misery for what he would have done, and so he calls the Lighthouse and leaves a message about sun and God, and two days later, She calls the Lighthouse and leaves a message about love and loss and regret, and the Conquistador, to pay tribute to all that is possible, to redeem his wretched self, tracks me down, and offers me a choice, and I go to Atlanta where She too makes a choice, and that choice brings death to our child, and I know I'll never get right with what She felt She had to do, and I also know I love Her all the more for choosing the fiancé over me—for casting Herself as the final pearl in a long and lovely string of wrongs—and for seeing the Conquistador for what he is: a hero. Like Achilles. Like Job. (Like Her demonic father.) It's the rare person who can see this. (Like seeing phosphorescence in black water.) Nor will I condemn him, his willingness to betray me (I know he'd have fucked Her in that office if She'd have given him half a chance). How can I condemn him? I understand him, his craving for divinity. So much like my own. Nor will I stand in the fiancé's way. In fact, I'll go a step further: I will walk away. I will do as the man who laid his last nickel on a plank-wood bar for a hunk of dented brass; as the homeless lunatic who braved the wrath of black-lava demons for a glimpse of mystery; as the woman who furiously raked the dirt around her pines; I will sacrifice myself for them, for all of us. Because I see now that it's not about me, not me at ten, not me at thirty-three. I see that Raynard is wrong and the Conquistador is right—love is not a hangnail it is a sun, big as everything, worth all. I see, also, that tragedy is the foundation upon which love reigns, the torch to love's flame. And sacrifice, sacrifice for love, that is the cold dark breath without which the flame would go cold, would go black, forever.

I see this now.

And I see…

I think I see…

Smoke. Yes, smoke. The smoke, finally, is undeniable. And flames. That damn cigarette. There's a forest fire. She's started a fire.

Finally.

I bolt from the porch, around back of the house, and to the edge of the woods. It's still there, the shovel, beside the fox's grave. Nothing grows on it but the earth is packed solid and flat, and I believe it will last, I believe he'll be safe from scavengers, and I'm grateful I had a hand in that.

Smoke now obscures the treetops, and the air's acquired a familiar, pond-green bloat. And a silence that makes me think the birds have all fled until I see the hummingbird—the hummingbirds—there must be twenty though it's hard to call numbers with them because they are so small. One could be twenty. When a hummingbird wants to move, it reappears.

Move. Past the pool and down my gravel spur. I spot the dugout where Her convertible landed and shoved off—where, minutes ago, She must have flicked Her cigarette, kindling this conflagration, then gunned it upwards through Redwoods and the dissonant soundtrack of babydoll rap.

Move. To the paved sidewinder road which I follow for maybe a quarter of a mile and then veer onto a fire trail that leads into a maze of fire trails where I ran once and only once. I don't know one trail from the next but that doesn't matter; I know which ones lead up.

Up. Sweat breaks. Breath comes sooty so I doff my shirt and tie it around my nose and mouth. Uninjured, I crutch my gait with the shovel; it clangs against the brick-hard dirt. I lower my head and follow it, the dirt, as if the dry cracks were lines in a map leading to a place I've prefigured. Vaguely I notice a bankturn, a steepening, a left-boot scuff and slip and rocks tumbling down a nightlike gorge. Profoundly I see the chasms this heat has cut in the earth as they pass beneath my feet. I lean into a steep and rise and lift my head to find oaks and pines have given way to redwoods, their unchecked bulk, their mastodon skin, their forever dusk through which I wind. Up through a place not made for me. My likes.

Clang goes the shovel. Coming through! Clang clang.

I don't know which is worse—this baked shirt singeing my mouth and nose, smarting my cheeks, or nothing between me and the heat. I do know this: the heat means I'm getting closer.

Eyes on the ground but the point of view here is not made for me. The point of view is a treetop view, downcast, and I'm tiny, segmenting over a golden floor of sparking needles, past folds of bark painful to the touch, fissures seeping smoke, and I'm high as a spire in a monster-throated wind and I'm low and I'm high and I'm stripping my shirt from my face the better to breathe, breathe, breathe so slow don't gasp don't fan the metal in the mouth and I'm low, I'm crawling beneath the cosmos smoke that's so low now it's almost firmly in position but I'm not so low I can't feel the lift, the scruff of the neck pick-up, the rise and summit and collapse to a burning floor that's hot, too hot, not made for me though maybe if I curl real small, too small to see, He'll let me be, He won't…look.

Squint through flooded eyes at the fire making its way my way across the floor of this promontory, flat somehow, through this mastodon stand, this burning cathedral in which I am naked to the waist, wet and gleaming, with prickling knuckles and hotshocked face but…

Stand up.

Find Him where He's been hiding all these years I've been alone with my divinity, this dead divinity, nothing for it to resonate against but Her, and She's gone please show Yourself now for the fire's raining through branches, the fire's groping for my face, the fire's tapping at my toes.

Backstep.

Bastard.

Whack of the century's what I'm thinking. Who cares if it's futile or flawed? I'm thinking burn me from front and back but I'll get a few good whacks in before the finish. I'm thinking why this absence in me if not for the removal of You? Why the removal? Why leave behind desire? Joke? Here's a joke: a shovel. Here's a shovel too hot to hold but ha ha, look, I'm hoisting it. I'm gonna swing it too, only my eyes are tight-squeezed shut against the heat. My whole body, in fact. Hard to fight in such a position. Do anything. But listen.

To the cymbal-fizz of needles, the high and the fallen. The breathtaking snap of branches severing and their burning soprano dive. Basso profundo wind. And the kisses. Slack-lipped, hungry, smack and suck and moan. All over everything even me, maybe, in such a position it's hard to know where you stand. What's to know? Now. What's to know now.

The sound of abandon. Listen.

Kisses.

Moans.

Talons.
In.
Chest.
Lifting.
Me.
Let them.
I am.
Lift you.
They are.
You are.
Out There.
So.
Light.
So
Vast.
Whump.
Suck.
Wonk.
Me.
Punk.
You.
Spiraling.
Spiraling.
Scared.
Very.
Awed.
Yes.
Humbled.
So.
Again?
Please.
Now.
Wait.
Now.
Oh.

Inward.

Downward.

Down.

Coming down.

In the heat.

Burning face and hands and feet and—.

Now, punk, lay your shovel down. Your little joke. Lay it down gently and proffer your first bow. Now rise. Fire's in back and front but you can still step to the side, now. Step. Keep your eyes shut for the fire's greater than you, greater than now. Step, step. Get out of the heat.

So I do. I go sideways. At flame's widening edge, I pause. Listen and look. Then down. Down fire trails to the paved road to the gravel road to the Glamshack.

And I'm standing above the fox's grave. I'm leaning over. I'm looking at dirt. I take a slow, smoke-bitten breath. Realease it with a rasp. Take another. Stand up straight. Peer through this shutter of pines at my pool, the deck chair still in the same mid-recline position as twelve days ago, when it hosted Her, naked, purple nipples and orange toes, cape to my bull my love Her skin my sun Her smile my moon all radiating, still, through these raging environs in this sparky mist don't move, don't interfere or She will vanish, don't look at that rosemary bush just come alight or it will ash.

I don't. I close my eyes. And understand that what got me to lay down my shovel, bow and sidle out of the conflagration up in my redwoods wasn't me. It was Her. That was Her urging. I know because of the place it came from: deep in my seabelly. I feel it now. Or rather, I hear it, Her; I hear Her. Only Her voice doesn't sound like the sexy Southern Siren I know. This voice is wide and warm and arrives in waves. She actually sounds like She loves me as She asks me what I see. I've got my eyes closed, I say. She says: what do you see? I say fire. She says open your eyes, tell me what you see. I say fire. She says, baby, fire of fire.

Acknowledgements

Thank you to the late James Salter, whose guidance and support helped me stay the course; to Marilynne Robinson, who made it O.K. to stand apart; to Leland Cheuk, whose brilliance made this book better; to Chris Offutt, from whom I learned revision; to Josh Kendall, who went to bat for this book; to the late William Styron, whose novel, *Sophie's Choice*, emboldened me to integrate the heroic, and tragic, story of the Plains Indian Wars; to the late Evan S. Connell, whose majestic nonfiction book, *Son of the Morning Star*, provided critical Indian Wars material, as well as inspiration.

About the Author

Paul Cohen's fiction has been published in *Tin House, Hypertext, Five Chapters,* and *Eleven Eleven.* He was a finalist in the Black Warrior Review Fiction Contest and his novel-in-progress *The Sleeping Indian* was named a finalist for the 2016 Big Moose Prize from Black Lawrence Press. His nonfiction has appeared in the *New York Times Magazine, Village Voice, Details,* the *Christian Science Monitor* and others. Cohen earned an MFA from the Iowa Writers' Workshop, where he was awarded a teaching scholarship as well as the Prairie Lights Prize for Fiction (judged by Ethan Canin). He has taught writing at UC Berkeley Extension, the University of San Francisco MFA program and the University of Iowa, and has guest lectured at California College of the Arts. He lives in Boulder, Colorado.

7.13
BOOKS